CODE OF IRON

Adler snorted. "The first thing, Billy boy, is that half the men I've killed were faster than me, and damn near all of them were better shots. What I had over them was an edge. And that is that I am always prepared to kill a man.

"I want you to think about that. Lay awake at night and study on it, son. It'll save your life. An awful lot of men will go into a gunfight and not want to hurt the other man. That makes them slow to pull the trigger no matter how fast they draw. I've had men stand in front of me with their guns drawn and look in my eyes and know I was going to kill them and they still couldn't bring themselves to shoot. Seen it more than once. So what you got to do, boy, is make peace with yourself over the fact that you can pull that trigger and send a bullet into a human person's gut. You got to be willing to make him bleed. You got to be willing to make them die. You want the dying to be done by him, not by you."

Adler spat.

"And if you can't live with it, you got no damned business wearing a gun."

MAN
ON THE
BORDER

DAVE AUSTIN

BERKLEY BOOKS, NEW YORK

MAN ON THE BORDER

A Berkley Book / published by arrangement with the author

PRINTING HISTORY
Berkley edition / April 2004

For information address: The Berkley Publishing Group, a division of Penguin Group (USA) Inc., 375 Hudson Street, New York, New York 10014.

ISBN: 0-425-19523-6

BERKLEY®
Berkley Books are published by The Berkley Publishing Group, a division of Penguin Group (USA) Inc., 375 Hudson Street, New York, New York 10014. BERKLEY and the "B" design are trademarks belonging to Penguin Group (USA) Inc.

PRINTED IN THE UNITED STATES OF AMERICA

10 9 8 7 6 5 4 3 2 1

ONE

"GET him now, head him. Head him. Quick!"

Billy stood in his stirrups and leaned forward, swirling the loop above his head. He reined closer to the steer and threw, his rope sailing straight at the head of the steer already caught at the heels by Leon's handmade riata.

The steer bawled and tossed its head, a string of snot flying straight up and sparkling in the sunlight.

Billy reined his horse hard to the left. Leon's mount was already coming to a sliding stop.

Dust and bits of ground litter flew, churned by three sets of hoofs as the two men and two horses tried to bring the one wild and spooky crossbred steer under control.

Billy felt the tug of resistance even though his rope was tied fast to the horn of the saddle that had been his father's.

The steer hit the end and turned its head and Billy heard a shout from behind.

The loop, wrapped only on the muzzle of the steer, slipped free as the steer pulled sulkily back from it.

Without that resistance, the horse became unbalanced and staggered in one direction while the steer fell the other way, sprawling onto its side.

The steer toppled, rolled, and wildly kicked. It managed to free Leon's rope from one hock and kicked again. Leon's horse was braced and setting back against the rope, and that helped pull the other hind leg out of the loop.

The steer scrambled to its feet and bolted back into the safety of the thick, thorny brush they had just chased it out of.

"Damn you, boy, you've let the sonuvabitch get away, and now he's riled. We won't never get him outa there now an' it's your damn fault, you useless little piece o' shit."

Billy's resentment rose hot and ugly, but he kept his tongue. He'd learned a long time ago that if he sassed Leon he was not the only one who would pay. The man was snake-mean and when angry took his venom out on Billy's mother too. Billy could stand a thrashing. God knows he'd had enough practice at it. But he could not abide the thought of this heavy-handed son of a bitch thumping on his mother again. She'd had more than enough practice too, and he wanted to cause her no more pain.

Two more months. That was all the longer he had to put up with this anyhow. In two more months Billy Delisle would turn twenty-one, and the place would become his by right of inheritance.

Then it would be his choice if Leon Soames stayed or went. And there wasn't much doubt about what he would choose.

Soames would be on his way down the road before sundown on Billy's birthday. *Without* Billy's mother, dammit.

They hadn't talked about it, Billy and her, but he knew she was as fed up with Soames as he was. The man was a womanizer and an abuser. He would beat up on anyone weaker than him and toady to anyone stronger. But the strong had better watch their backsides afterward because Soames was as sneaky as he was mean. Fairness didn't mean anything to him; nastiness did.

Billy could hardly wait for that day to come. But until then, he was going to be on his extra-best behavior. From now until then, butter wouldn't melt in his mouth.

But Leon Soames better watch himself come that day because things were going to be a heap different come the time.

"Damn you, stop your lollygagging an' get that rope off'n the ground. We got better to do than lay about. Now move."

Billy did not trust himself to speak. He merely nodded. And began dragging his rope in, coiling it as he did so and building a new loop once he had it in hand.

They worked like that, catching a few and earmarking them before pushing them into the holding pen they'd built of brush and cactus, losing more. The ones that were lost were all lost from Billy's fault, at least to hear Leon tell it. The truth was that Billy no longer cared about that.

But he did care about catching all the beeves they could. The more they caught, the more they would sell, and the more sold, then the more the earnings.

And Lord knows they needed all the cash money they could bring in. They got by, but there never seemed to be anything left over. It would be nice if once, just once, they had enough money in hand that Billy's mother could have herself cloth to make a new dress or silk flowers to freshen up her Sunday hat.

They worked until it was too dark to find the cattle that were skulking in the brush, until the dusk leached away what little color there was in the dusty growth and on the red and black and speckled hides of the cattle. Finally, Leon grudgingly turned his mount back toward the home place and without bothering to tell Billy he was going, put the animal into a jog homeward.

Soames might be a son of a bitch, but he was a hard worker. Billy had to give him that. And he was no drunkard. He would have a little nip now and then when they rode in to town, but the man was not a drinker. Of course, that also meant he didn't have the excuse of being whiskey-addled when he went to hitting on Billy or his mother. Billy attributed that trait to the man's innate meanness.

They rode back in silence, Billy trailing along behind the big bay that Soames preferred, and Leon called out when they were within hailing distance of the clapboard house with the breezeway between its two halves.

"Here, boy. Do my horse. And mind you do him right," Soames said, handing Billy his reins.

There were a number of things Billy could have said in response to that. Quite a number of things he would like to have said. Instead, for his mother's sake, he kept his lip buttoned and took the damn reins.

Soames walked around to the side of the house and poured himself some clean water to wash in. Billy knew good and well he would have used the whole pitcher, leaving Billy dirty water to use or a trip to the well for fresh.

Which meant he would have to pump water. No way was he going to use Leon Soames's leavings.

Billy fed both horses and brushed down his own—if Leon wanted the bay curried he was welcome to do it himself—then went to the well so he could wash. By the time he got inside, Leon was halfway done with his meal and had all the remaining corn dodgers piled along the edge of his plate so there wouldn't be any left over for Billy.

His mother gave Billy a nervous look, but didn't say anything. Billy figured she probably had a few of the corn cakes laid by in the warming oven, for she knew how much he loved them. She would bring them out later, after Leon was snoring. He gave his mother a kiss and a hug and helped himself to a seat at the far end of the table from Leon, then reached for the bowl of pinto beans and hog jowl.

TWO

"I left food for you in the warming oven. There's coffee in the pot. Leave the dishes when you're done. I'll wash them when we get home."

Billy overheard his mother's instructions as he came in to tell her the wagon was hitched and ready. He permitted himself a small smile in response to a memory from long ago.

Leon never tried to keep his mother and him from going to church. Not anymore he didn't. He'd kept them home from the circuit rider's monthly meetings just once. That was early in the marriage when Billy was just a sprout, and before they knew how quick Soames was to use his fists.

The man slapped Billy's mom and told her she didn't have his permission to go off for some foolishness like preaching. They'd stayed home that day. But Soames's life must not been very pleasant until the next meeting day.

Billy was not entirely sure what-all was involved in his mother's retaliation. All he'd been sure of at the time was the brittle coldness that his mom showed her new husband all day every day. He was pretty sure there was more to it than just that, of course, and whatever it was, it cured Soames of his Sunday morning bossiness.

Truth was that Billy doubted his mother would have the gumption to stand up to the man again these years later, but the lesson Soames got then seemed to have taken right well, and there were no more complaints about the two of them going off for that one day each month.

"We're ready, Mama," Billy said as he picked up the wicker hamper his mother had packed heavy with their lunch and dinner. She'd stayed up late the night before cooking and wrapping and fussing over it. The meal a person laid out ready to share with friends and neighbors and strangers alike was important to the womenfolk, and his mother would not want to be shamed in front of the rest of the worshippers.

"Good-bye, mister," his mother said.

It was odd, but Billy had never heard her refer to Leon any other way than "mister." She never spoke to him by name, nor used any of the small endearments he could remember her and his father saying to one another.

Billy loaded the hamper into the back of the wagon, then handed his mother up onto the seat bench. He'd folded a saddle blanket and laid it there to pad the seat for her as there was no upholstery. A pair of lap robes were stashed underneath the seat along with a couple slickers, but he doubted any of those would be needed at this warm, dry time of year.

Of course, most any time of year was warm and dry in

the south of New Mexico Territory, but there could be exceptions, and the exceptions could turn out to be downright thrilling. Uncomfortable too if you weren't prepared for them.

Billy ran around to the driver's side and scrambled into the wagon. He took up the lines and shook them to get the attention of the old cobs that had been retired to light driving duty, then set a course for the big brush arbor along Whelan Creek where the Sunday meetings were always held.

THE preaching had already started when Billy and his mother arrived. He helped his mother out of the rig; then she went on to choose a place on the crude benches that were built by someone years back. He led the team over to the area that was set aside as a wagon park, unhitched and hobbled the horses, and turned them loose to pick at the lush grass that grew along the banks of the creek.

He threw a lap robe over the food hamper to keep the sun heat off it, then went to join his mother.

The preaching was fiery and the singing vigorous, and Billy was sure it was all of great interest and importance. Or would have been had he been able to pay attention to any of it.

His mother, bless her, had been thoughtful enough to choose a spot just one bench back and a little to the right of the place where the Foresters were sitting. From there he was able to get a good look at Edith Forester.

She knew it too. He could tell by the flush of dark red that started on her neck a moment after he took his seat. The blush spread upward onto her cheek, and her posture went rigid as she struggled to keep from being distracted. After a minute or so, though, she just couldn't help it. She turned half around in her seat so she could peek at him. She blushed all the more furiously when she caught him staring at her.

But she was smiling even so.

Billy grinned, his chest full and his heart joyous.

Life, he thought, was good.

And it was going to get even better.

THREE

IT was sometime past noon when they broke for dinner, everyone taking their blankets and picnic hampers and heading for the shade along the creek. There must have been a hundred, hundred fifty or more people there to spend the day listening to the preaching, eating, gossiping, in general having a fine old time.

Billy kept an eye on Mrs. Forester and made sure him and his mother's hamper traveled in the same direction. He got the blanket and hamper situated for his mother, then discovered to his great consternation that Edith was missing from the Forester family group.

"She took Jason upstream to play," his mother said in response to Billy's disappointed confusion.

He raised an eyebrow. "Why do you say they've gone to play?"

"Because if it was some other sort of business they

would've gone downstream, wouldn't they? Go on now. I'll set our things out, then go have a word with Martha Garrison. I want to see how she is doing."

Billy kissed his mother on the cheek and took off through the woods upstream.

He found a yammering clutch of young children in that direction, Edie's little brother among them. Billy went a little further upstream, past the children, then circled back from that unexpected direction so he could slip up behind Edie and surprise her. He tugged her pigtail, then with a whoop turned and ran.

Edie immediately gave loudly vocal chase, shouting threats of bloody mayhem just as soon as she caught him.

The two raced into the woods and out of sight from the others.

Billy stopped and whirled. He was no longer laughing.

Nor was Edie when she flung herself into his arms.

They did not know if this ruse would still fool anyone or not, and they did not really care.

Edie's kiss was passionate and as yearning as Billy's. "I've missed you," she whispered when finally they paused for breath.

"Me too."

"I love you."

"Me too."

"You love you too?" she teased.

"Naw. I don't need to. I got you to do that for me."

Edie laughed, and he kissed her again.

After a few minutes, when his breathing became too ragged and serious for comfort, the two pulled reluctantly apart lest they push temptation too far. Billy took her by the hand and led her to the trunk of a fallen tree. It was a spot they'd discovered years earlier and still thought of as their own. He carefully brushed the wood free of leaves and bits of twigs, then helped Edie to a seat before he settled close beside her.

"Are you all right?" she asked.

He nodded.

"He isn't bothering you?" She did not have to say the name for him to know who she meant.

"No more'n usual." He smiled. "I can put up with anything, y'know, for a couple lousy months. Then we'll talk to your pa and post the notices. Quick as we can manage it, girl, you'll be Mrs. William Delisle. How does that sound to you?"

She sighed. "Do you want to know something? I practice writing that out every which way. Mrs. William Delisle. Mrs. Billy Delisle. Edie Delisle. Mrs. Edith Forester Delisle." She laughed. "I'll bet I've used up a box and a half of chalks just writing my new name. Then I swipe the slate clean again and start over just for the fun of it."

"Don't you do any studying anymore?"

"Of course I do. I study on what it's going to be like being Mrs. Billy Delisle." She leaned forward and kissed him.

Billy sat back, happier than he had known it was ever possible to be. He looked at her. Which was one of his very favorite things to do anyway. My, but he was lucky. So very lucky to have the most beautiful girl in the whole of New Mexico. In the whole vast country west of the Mississippi. Heck, the most beautiful girl in the whole wide world probably.

Edie was sixteen now, and would be finishing up her

schooling just about the same time Billy turned twenty-one and could inherit. She was slim as a rake handle, with huge gray eyes and long, very long pale blond hair and soft, very soft lips and sparkling white teeth and dimples. He loved her dimples. But then he loved everything about her. Had for as long as he could remember just about. Well, since she was twelve or thirteen anyway; before that she'd seemed like just another kid underfoot and he hadn't paid her much mind. Edie swore that she'd been in love with him since she was five. But he suspected she might've exaggerated about that.

Not that it mattered. The point was that the both of them were in love now and always would be and soon—not soon enough, but soon—they would be married.

Billy reached out and lightly touched Edie's cheek. He ran his fingertips over her throat and across her lips and onto her eyelids, looking at her, marveling at his great good fortune . . . loving her.

He stroked her hair and then her pigtail—Edie's mother insisted she wear her hair like that, trying to keep her a child, Billy thought—and wondered how it would feel when someday he could run his fingers through her loose hair. He'd never once seen her with her hair let down and full, and there was something about that thought that excited him.

He swallowed hard and snatched his hand away as if he were doing something wrong, having thoughts like that.

There was nothing he would do to harm or to dishonor Edie. Never.

"I love you, Mrs. Delisle," he whispered.

"I love you, Mr. Delisle," she answered.

"Edith Jane, you'd best come. Pa's looking for you and

he'll get hoppin' mad if he finds out you been up here with some ol' boy."

Billy and Edie pulled suddenly apart, and Billy felt the beginnings of a blush warm his neck and cheeks.

"That may be," Edie said, "but Pa won't find out nothing." She gave her little brother a syrupy sweet and entirely phony smile. "Will he, Jason?"

"Not from me he won't. Huh-uh, no, ma'am."

"I didn't think so, else mama just might find out what happened to that crock of milk last week."

"I said there won't nobody find out nothing from me, did'n I?"

They stood up, and Edie took the time to give Billy a long, lingering, loving kiss. Even with Jason standing right there all bug-eyed and incredulous.

Lordy, but he was one happy, lucky fellow, Billy exulted as the three walked back toward the picnic area.

FOUR

BILLY hated little bitty buttons, danged if he didn't. His fingers just couldn't get around them the way they ought. He fiddled and fumbled for a minute or so, then gave up and found the sewing box where his mother kept her thread and needles and a dozen other sorts of female things.

The particular thing he wanted . . . ah! There. In triumph he brought out the button hook she used to put her Sunday shoes on. The hook worked every bit as well on a collar button.

He finished fastening the fresh collar to his shirt, and reached for a length of dark silk that his mother had cut off the hem of her best dress so she could make a necktie for him. He wasn't very good at tying it. But he could manage. After a fashion. He looped it around his neck and headed for the door so he could step outside and use the mirror over the washstand.

"Where the hell d'you think you're going?" Leon de-manded when Billy came out wearing his boiled shirt and suit pants.

"Town," Billy told him.

Leon dropped the hoof he'd been cleaning and scowled. The bay horse shook itself like a dog coming out of water and swished its tail a couple times.

"You can't go to town today. You got to cut more cedar for fence posts."

"No. What I *got* to do today is go to town. To the court-house, to be precise about it. Today's my birthday, Leon, and it's time I claim my inheritance."

"An' what inheritance would that be? Boy!" He bore down on the word "boy," making it sound nasty and in-sulting.

"You know good and well what inheritance I have com-ing to me. My pap left me this place. It says right there in his Last Will an' Testament that he obliges me to take care of my mama . . . which he knew I'd do anyhow . . . but the land and the livestock all come to me."

Billy paused and considered for a moment, then added, "Something that might be of interest to you, Mr. Soames, is that my pap's will don't say nothing about taking care of you. From now on, mister, you'll treat my mama right or you'll find your ass riding the grub line. I won't turn you out. Not without cause. But I'm telling you plain, you treat my mama right or I won't be responsible for what happens to you after."

Billy expected Leon to blow up. Maybe even come after him. Instead, the man only snorted and shook his head. He took up the bay's reins and walked off leading the horse and laughing.

That was a relief. It was something he'd worried about telling to Leon, and now it turned out all that fretting had been for nothing. Not that he was complaining.

He began to feel better. Much better.

And began thinking all over again about Edith Forester.

He would go to the courthouse first this morning. But then afterward, perhaps he would ride over to Edie's place and have that talk with her father. That too was something he'd been dreading almost as much as he'd been looking forward to.

He intended to ask Edie's father for permission to court her. To post the banns. To hold the biggest, happiest, grandest wedding this old county ever saw.

Smiling and trembling at one and the same time, Billy Delisle finished tying his necktie and went back inside to get his suit coat and the will that needed recording at the courthouse.

FIVE

"MAMA."

"Yes, dear?"

"Did you move the Will an' Testament?"

"It's in the steel box the same as always."

"No, ma'am, it isn't. I just looked."

"Then look again, dear."

"I looked twice. Are you sure you didn't move it?"

"I haven't touched it in . . . I don't recall the last time I saw it. Two or three years probably."

"Mama, it isn't *here*!"

He fumbled, frantic now, through the few papers his father had kept in the flat, black enameled steel box. Marriage certificate. Baptism certificates for all of them. Deed. Several satisfactions of notes from back when his father first stocked the place, and again some years after when he upgraded the bloodlines with a shipment of bulls brought down from Indiana. Old photographs: Billy's parents on their wedding day; his father and a dozen other members of his cavalry troop in the field, that one taken during a campaign against the Cheyenne; the house, taken before the outbuildings were completed; their first windmill and stock tank; Billy in a bonnet and ruffled dress, probably taken before he could walk on his own.

But there was no Last Will and Testament.

No matter how many times he looked, no matter how desperately he shuffled through all his parents' most important documents and photographs, there simply was no will.

SIX

BILLY damn near killed his horse getting the twenty-four miles from home to town. He probably should have been ashamed of himself, but wasn't. He'd had to slow down for the last five or six miles, and every moment of the ride he'd wanted to screw his face into a tight nub hung off the front of his head and bawl like a baby. He hadn't, of course. He was twenty-one years old now and a man grown. But dammit, he'd sure felt like it.

He knew what happened. Of course he did. Knew that that was the reason that damned Leon Soames just laughed when Billy said he was going to the courthouse to get the deed put in his name.

Leon, that double-dipped son of a bitch, had taken the will out of the box—it was never locked, never hidden, for after all it was only family that would've had access to it—and done something with it.

Probably burned it, Billy figured. There would have been no point to hiding it. If he did that Billy or, more likely, his mother could come across it and take it to the courthouse even years from now.

No, Soames almost certainly destroyed the will. Maybe used it to start a fire. No one would have noticed or paid the least bit of attention. Who would have thought it?

Now . . . Billy did not know what would happen now. Did not have any idea what his rights were. Or his mother's rights.

His mother! She was married to Leon. Worse, she was thoroughly cowed by him. He'd beaten her so often in the past that she never stood up to him anymore. Whatever he said, whatever he wanted, it was better than being beat on again. Billy didn't even know if she would be willing to testify to what the missing will had said.

For that matter, he didn't know if he would ask her to testify should it come to that. If she said anything against Soames, she would be setting herself up for a hellacious beating. She would know that and so did Billy. Even if he thought she would testify, he didn't know if it would be right to ask her to do so.

Oh, *damn* that man anyway!

He reached town with his horse still alive. Lathered and trembling and near to collapsing. But alive.

He stopped first at the public livery and turned the horse over to Howard Lipp.

"Geez, Bill, what'd you do to this animal? Don't you know any better'n to ride a horse that hard?"

"Sorry. Take care of him, would you, please. You know what to do for him. And when I get done with what I got to do here, I may need to borrow one of your horses to get home on."

"You aren't gonna put a saddle on any animal o' mine, young man, if you think you can do to him what you done to this one."

"It won't happen again, Mr. Lipp. I promise. Now please. Just take care of my horse, please. There's stuff I got to do. Important stuff."

"I should hope so. Huh! The idea of riding a horse this hard . . ."

Billy turned, leaving Howard talking to himself at the front of his big barn, and headed at a trot toward the courthouse.

"NOW, William, you know better," Dave France, the clerk of court, told him. "I cannot file a document that does not exist. I couldn't do that even if I had personally seen the paper and knew its contents. Much the less am I going to grant you a change of ownership just because you claim such a will exists. Or once did exist." France shook his head. "You should know better than that. Really."

"Who should I talk to then?" Billy asked.

"My recommendation would be for you to hire a lawyer. A really good one. One of those fancy Santa Fe lawyers maybe. One that knows the politicians even better than he knows the law. That's my advice to you, William."

"What if I don't have the money for that?"

"Then I'd say that in a case like this, any lawyer is better than no lawyer."

"How about the sheriff? D'you think he could do anything for me?"

"I doubt it."

"That will was stolen outa the box where my folks always kept it."

"I could explain a few things to you, William, but I can see you wouldn't pay any mind to me anyway. Go ahead. See the sheriff. He ought to be upstairs in his office this time of day. Go talk to him."

"Yes, sir. Thank you, Mr. France."

Billy took the stairs two at a time on his way up to the county sheriff's office.

SEVEN

SHERIFF Joe Kauf shook his head. "Billy, there's not a damned thing I can do here. Dave already told you the way it is. Without some document to go on, there is nothing he can do and nothing I can do. The only thing I'd disagree with is him telling you to get a lawyer. That would be money thrown away."

"But Sheriff, that will was stolen. Leon took it out of the box . . . it wasn't any secret what was in there, you see . . . and he did something with it. Probably burned it or tore it up or anyhow destroyed it one way or another."

"Know that for a fact, do you?"

"Of course I do. Who else would've done it?"

"And you have proof to go along with that assertion?"

"Well . . . not proof. Exactly. But I *know* he did it."

"Knowing something isn't good enough, Billy. You have to prove it. Did anyone see Leon take the document?"

"No, sir, I expect not. I didn't find out it was gone until this morning when I went to get it to record."

Kauf shook his head again. "Son, the only glimmer of hope I can think of would be for you to talk with the lawyer who drew up that will. He might've saved a copy in his files, or at the least might remember what your pa said he should put in it. Do you know who the lawyer was?"

"There wasn't no lawyer, sir. Pap wrote it out in his own hand and signed it."

"Were there witnesses?"

"I think there might have been. But I wouldn't know who."

Kauf grunted. "Most generally all a witness can attest to is the validity of the signature anyway. A document like that, it's a private sort of thing. A witness wouldn't normally read it. Just see who was signing it."

"Yes, sir, I know that."

"Billy, I don't think you have a leg to stand on. I think you haven't a hope in the world of ever seeing that will executed the way you say your pa wanted done."

"You mean Leon owns the ranch, is that it?"

"In a nutshell . . . yes. It belonged to your mother. Whatever belonged to your mother now belongs to him. That's just the way it is."

"But, sir, it's . . . it's *wrong!*"

"Billy, the fact of the matter is, the law has nothing to do with simple right and wrong. It has to do with the law. Period. And in this situation, with nothing but your word to claim your pa wanted the place to go to you, you just don't have the law on your side. I'm sorry. But you don't."

"Can I file a complaint against him? For stealing?"

"Certainly. Anybody can complain about anything. That's the law too. But I have to warn you, when you lose . . . and I can promise you that you would lose . . . you would lay yourself open for a countersuit. You could end up owing Leon everything you ever make or do or become, your whole life long. Billy, if you insist on filing a complaint, it is my bounden duty to accept that and write it out. But I surely hope you won't do anything so foolish. Bad as it may be . . . and I reckon it is mighty bad to lose everything your pa worked for . . . you're going to have to live with the way things are and not the way you'd like them to be. Go on home. Nothing will have changed. You and Leon and your mama will still have the place, and everything will be just like it was last year and last month and yesterday. There just won't be any changes, that's all."

Billy felt numb, drained. He did not know where to turn next. Go home, Sheriff Kauf said. It was odd, but the place where he'd spent pretty much his whole life no longer seemed home to him. He felt now like he had no home. No future. No nothing.

He turned toward the stairs, much more slowly this time than he'd been coming up.

"Billy."

"Yes, sir?"

"I'll not countenance any violence. I want you to know that."

"No, sir." That thought, in truth, had not occurred to him. "I don't expect that would solve anything anyway."

"No, it surely wouldn't."

Happy twenty-first birthday, Billy told himself rather bitterly as he walked slowly back toward the livery.

EIGHT

HIS mother said nothing when he told her what happened in town. Nothing. It felt like a betrayal. At the very least she could have gotten mad along with him. Could have said *some*thing.

She knew as well as he did that her husband was the one who took the will. The law might need proof, but no one else would. Leon took it and that was all there was to it. Took the will and took the land. Took the house, the cattle, the horses . . . everything.

And his mother said nothing at all when he told her.

She just . . . stood there. Looked at him with that dull, empty expression she'd had for the past . . . he tried to remember the last time she'd really shown any interest in anything. Anything other than the monthly preaching and psalm-singing, that is. She would cry at those times. But as for the rest of the time, it had been . . . three years? Four?

She'd never been all that demonstrative. But at least she'd laughed some. Fretted some. Cared some. Now . . . she didn't seem to care much about anything at all.

Funny how he'd never really thought about that before. The change, he thought now, had come about so slowly that he hadn't really noticed.

Now . . . now she could at least have given a da<u>mn</u> that her own husband stole the inheritance from her only child.

Billy took a handful of cold leftover corn dodgers from a plate on the stove and went outside to sulk.

NINE

"THERE'S three, four hours of good daylight yet. Go cut some cedar posts. We got fencing to build."

"Go to hell," Billy told him.

"Don't sass me, boy. I said you're to go cut posts. Now git!" Soames balled his right hand into a fist and advanced on Billy with smug satisfaction writ large on his face. "Or is there somethin' you want to say to me, boy? Anything you wanta make a smart comment about?"

Billy watched Leon's approach with hatred but, curiously, no fear at all.

It had been years since the last time Leon touched him. Truth to tell, it had been years since the man last had to. Billy had accepted his role and quietly, patiently bided his time for that twenty-first birthday.

Well, that day had come now and was fast going and nothing was changed. Or almost nothing. Billy's contempt

for his mother's husband had crystallized now and solidi-
fied. It slid past loathing and was unadulterated hate, and
that would never change now no matter what.

He recognized that as he watched Soames approach
him, and for the first time there was no room in him for
fear. Other feelings drove the fear from him.

"Get up, boy. Hitch that wagon and grab a saw. You got
work to do."

Soames stood in front of him, both fists balled, the
knuckles of both hands planted onto his hips, his feet
spread shoulder-width apart as he braced, ready to pound
Billy if this defiance continued.

Billy silently nodded, and Soames seemed to accept this
as the humble acquiescence he was accustomed to receiving from Billy and from Billy's mother.

The gesture, however, was but Billy's own affirmation
of what was to come.

Leon Soames outweighed him by a good forty pounds
or more and stood at least three inches taller. Soames was
older, stronger, and far more experienced. He had fought
with half the men in the county and whipped nearly all of
them. No one stood up to him nowadays. No one.

Billy lifted himself off the rat-proof grain bin where
he'd been sitting and stood there for a moment.

He took a deep, slow breath.

And whipped his right fist knuckles forward into Leon's
breadbasket. He hit the SOB just as hard as he knew how,
then lowered his head and did it again and again and again,
driving the air from the older man's lungs and keeping up
a continuous pounding that prevented Soames from being
able to draw a complete breath.

He kept on pounding after Soames dropped to his

knees, changing only his target now that Leon's face was at a convenient level for those low, driving, flesh-splitting, pulverizing blows.

Kept it up even after Soames collapsed completely and Billy had to drop onto his knees, dropping onto Leon's chest, distantly conscious of the dull and meaty sound of ribs breaking.

Pounding. Pounding. Battering. Until exhaustion made him cease pummeling the unresisting, unconscious man who was his mother's husband.

Billy had to lean on the side of the grain bin to pull himself upright again, and he staggered when he tried to walk back to the house, leaving Soames stretched out on the barn floor with his head in the red mud made of his own blood.

"I'm done here, Mama," he announced once he made it inside. "Pack me what chuck you can spare and roll up my bed. I'm gonna take the gray gelding. If he wants to file charges 'bout that, he knows where to find the sheriff."

"Son, I . . ."

Billy just looked at her. Anything she wanted to say she could've said earlier. She'd made her choices then. He didn't want to hear about them now.

After a moment, his mother must have seen both his disgust and his determination. Mutely, she turned into the kitchen alcove that was her place and her purpose and began to do what her son said she must.

TEN

IT was strange. This morning he'd felt man-grown and capable. Tonight he felt like a scared little boy.

Instead of owning his own place, tonight he had no home at all. No home. As good as no family.

No job. No prospects. No . . . oh, Lordy. It was bad enough not having a home. Now he had to tell Edie. And Mr. Forester.

Uh, maybe telling Mr. Forester could wait. He was in no hurry to open that can of worms.

He rode into the Foresters' yard just about the time the last of the daylight was fading from the sky. It was a beautiful evening, clear and fine, with darkness off to the east and violet, rose, purple, and gold streaking the horizon to the west. Somehow, that made it all the more difficult. He might've felt better if the rest of the world matched his gloomy prospects.

Mr. Forester's dogs set up a howling as Billy came nigh, and a moment later there was a spill of yellow lamplight onto the porch as the front door was pulled open. "Who's out there?"

"It's just me, Mr. Forester."

"Billy? Is that you? Is there something wrong over to your place?"

There was plenty wrong, but none of it was the sort of thing you went running to ask neighbors to fix. "No, sir. I just . . . I'd like to speak with Edith if I may, sir."

"Do you have any idea what time it is, Billy?"

"Pretty much, sir, yes. I . . . it's important."

Mr. Forester's shape, silhouetted dark against the brightness inside, withdrew from the doorway and was replaced with the slim figure of his daughter. And the bulkier shape of Edith's mother.

"Have you had your supper, Billy?" Mrs. Forester called out.

"No, ma'am."

"Would you come inside then? We have a little left over."

"I'm fine, ma'am, thank you."

"Nonsense. I won't take no for an answer. We can't have you go riding off from here hungry. Whatever would people think!"

"Yes, ma'am."

"In that case," he heard Mr. Forester say from inside, "you'd just as well unsaddle and put your horse in the corral. Make sure there's hay in the bunk."

"Yes, sir, thank you."

Edie came out onto the porch. "I'll go show him where everything is, Papa."

"He already knows where things are, Edith Jane."

"Yes, Papa." But she came out anyway, and her father didn't object, at least not that Billy could hear.

Jason came out too. And went scurrying promptly back when Edie bent and whispered something into his ear.

She came to him, and first glanced back to make sure neither of her folks was watching, then raised up and gave him a kiss. She linked her arm into his elbow and walked with him as he led the gray to the corral.

When Billy pulled his saddle, she frowned. "Are you going somewhere, Billy? Why do you have a bedroll with you? And those pokes of stuff? Is something wrong?"

He told her. Hard and abrupt. The thievery. The law. The fight. Everything. He managed to do it without breaking down and being unmanly about it. He was grateful for that small victory anyhow.

"Oh, Billy. Oh, dear." Edith pressed herself tight to his chest, her hair soft and fragrant under his chin. "Oh, my darling Billy."

He put his arms around her and patted her. He didn't know if that did anything to make her feel better, but it did a world of good for him to be able to be comforting someone else instead of feeling sorry for himself.

"What are you going to do now?"

"I . . . I don't know."

It was true. Awful. But true.

He hadn't thought a stitch nor a step further than getting away from Leon Soames's ranch—which he supposed it well and truly was now—and over here to Edith.

But as for the rest of this night . . . as for the rest of his life . . . he hadn't the least idea.

"I'm going to marry you," he heard himself say. "Just like we planned."

"But . . ."

"I'm going to find a way to support us. I'm going to take care of you. And I'm going to marry you. That's what I'm going to do."

"I love you, Billy Delisle."

"And I love you right back, Edith Forester."

She snuggled closer. "Edith Delisle," she whispered.

"Ma says his supper's ready," Jason piped up from no more than half a pace distant, causing both of them to jump like they'd been scalded.

ELEVEN

BILLY pushed his plate back. "Thank you, Miz Forester, but I couldn't hold another bite." She tried to induce him to have "just another bite," but he had no choice but to decline.

Mr. Forester stood. "Edith, you can wash the dishes for your mama. Billy, whyn't you come outside with me while they clean up in here."

"Yes, sir."

"Jason, help your sister with the dishes."

"But Pa . . ."

"What did I say?"

The protest died stillborn. Jason knew that tone of voice. He turned and hastened toward the copper sink and began to vigorously pump clean water into the rinse bucket, while Edith drew hot water from the reservoir on the side of the stove.

Billy followed Mr. Forester outside and along the porch to the rocking chair that Edith's father favored. "Sit down, Bill." He motioned toward the straight chair placed nearby while he himself took the rocker.

"Yes, sir."

"Smoke?"

"No, thank you."

"Chew?"

"No, sir."

"Drink hard spirits?"

"No, sir, can't say that I have."

"Consort with evil women, do you?"

"Mr. Forester, you know that I don't, else you would've heard about it and so would Edie."

"I suppose you're right about that." He took his time filling his pipe, then struck a sulphur-tipped match and lighted it with care. "I'm sorry to hear about your situation, Bill."

"Thank you, sir."

"Any idea what you will do now?"

"No, sir."

Forester grunted. "You can't stay here, of course. Even if I had work for you, it wouldn't be right for you to stay here. The whole county knows how you feel about my girl."

The whole county? Lordy. Billy hadn't even known until this minute that Mr. and Mrs. Forester knew.

"You aren't a bad boy, Bill. I expect you will make a good man someday."

There seemed plenty of sting in that praise. Someday. Which meant not now. Not yet.

"Mind if I ask you something?" Forester said.

"No, sir, go ahead."

"I noticed your hands are pretty well chopped up. Like as if you'd been hitting a barn wall. You haven't been doing anything like that, have you?"

"No, sir. Nor kicking dogs nor beating mules if that's what you're getting at."

Forester puffed on his pipe for a moment. The smoke from it smelled good. "Then what did happen to your hands? If you don't mind me asking."

"I expect that I hurt them when I hit Leon."

"Boy like you, you went an' hit Leon Soames, did you?"

"Yes, sir, and I'd do it again if I had to." He wasn't ashamed of it, dammit. Not after what Leon did to him. Billy kept his chin up and his eyes steady on Mr. Forester.

"I don't see any marks on you, Bill."

"No, sir, I expect I didn't give him any time to mark me none."

"I see." Again Forester stopped to puff a little. A slight breeze came up, sending the drifting smoke swirling into oblivion. The air was moving the other way so Billy could no longer smell it. "Know what I think, Bill?"

"No, sir."

"I think you have more sand in you than I'd been giving you credit for."

Billy didn't know quite what to say to that, so he kept his mouth shut.

"You don't look half tough enough to whip Leon. But I expect you went and did it anyway."

Again Billy kept his silence. But then what was he supposed to say? That he did look tough? Fact was, he didn't.

At all. He was light built and none too beefy, and had a schoolboy face and hair that he couldn't keep down.

"I like that," Mr. Forester said, which very nearly amazed Billy to the point that he could've fallen down if he wasn't already sitting. Until now he'd always sort of figured Mr. Forester to think of him as a nuisance. If he thought about him at all.

"I'd like to give you some advice, young man, seeing as your own daddy is dead. And that my girl is so sweet on you."

Billy felt himself blush.

"You'd best leave this country. And not just to keep clear of Leon, though I suspect that would be a pretty good idea too. The thing is, you aren't going to find much in the way of work around here." Forester smiled. "You can ride good enough, but I've seen you rope. You aren't ever going to draw wages as a top hand. And anyway, even top hands aren't set for family responsibilities." He paused. "Your intentions *are* honorable, aren't they?"

"Yes, *sir*, why, I . . ."

Forester waved him into silence. "You don't have to gild that lily any further, son. And I think I'd just as soon not have any details about just exactly what those intentions are, if you don't mind."

"Uh, no, sir." Billy agreed with that, all right.

"What I think you'd best do is go off and see what you can make of yourself. You have my permission to write to Edith while you're working that out."

"Thank you, sir. That's mighty generous of you." And so it was. He hadn't expected anything at all like this now that he was barely twenty-one and without prospects for the future.

Forester's pipe hissed and gurgled as the coal reached the last of the tobacco. Edith's father stood, stretched, then tapped the bowl of the pipe on the porch rail to knock the dottle onto the ground. Billy stood too.

"You can sleep in the shed over yonder tonight, Bill. You're welcome to take breakfast with us in the morning. Then I think it'd be best, for Edith's reputation and my peace of mind both, if you move on to find your way from here."

"Yes, sir. Thank you, Mr. Forester. Thank you very much."

"One more thing."

"Yes, sir?"

"I sleep light."

Billy did not immediately grasp what Forester was telling him. Then he realized and again felt the heat come into his ears. He sputtered, "I . . . I wouldn't never . . . really I . . ." But by then Forester was striding back down the porch. And closing the door firmly behind him once he was inside.

TWELVE

EL Paso took his breath away. Billy brought the gray to a stop at the crest of a hill, and sat there for a time just marveling at the huge, sprawling city. Cities, he supposed they really were, as the nearer was El Paso, which was in Texas, while on the far side of the Rio Grande, the city of Juarez was on Mexican territory.

It would have been impossible to miss finding El Paso, not only because all the roads led there, but also because the smoke from thousands of stoves and ovens built a gray column that was as good a marker as a weary traveler could hope to see.

There were . . . he could not begin to guess how many people there would be. Thousands. Maybe tens of thousands. The rooftops and tall brick buildings and low adobe walls stretched for miles upstream and downstream.

Billy had read about cities. But in truth, he'd never

imagined anything so huge as this. It took him a while to muster nerve enough to enter that teeming mass of commerce and humanity.

Finally, though, he nudged the gray forward again even though Billy's belly was aflutter with the butterflies of nervousness.

THE automobile spooked him. The gray horse was fine about it, plodding stolidly forward and paying no mind to the clattering, clanking, horseless contraption they encountered on a dusty El Paso street. But Billy almost jumped out of his skin at the sight of the thing.

Oh, he had read about them. Had even seen pictures. But somehow, he hadn't been prepared for the actual sight of one.

And his startled amazement at the automobile was nothing compared to what he saw downtown.

It was . . . well, it was sort of like a railroad car. Not a whole train, mind, but a single car. A passenger car of a long, boxy shape, with windows down both sides and padded benches for the people to ride on and a long cupola sort of thing perched on top of it for nearly the entire length of the car. It rode on regular railroad wheels, although they might have been of a slightly smaller size than on a regular rail car.

It ran on tracks that were laid right smack in the middle of the public street.

That much he could accept, all right.

But this rail car . . . it had no horses pulling it.

And it wasn't making that chug-chug, clatter-snort sound like the automobile did, nor was there any sign of a boiler or fire or any of the usual things one would associate with a railroad engine.

This car just . . . ran. On its own.

It was tethered for some reason to a cable that ran overhead, also down the middle of the street.

A long pole was hooked onto that cable and trailed along with the car.

Billy had no idea what that could be for. Certainly it wasn't to guide the thing as the rails would do that. And it wasn't strong enough to hold the car if for some reason it started to tip over. That rig was just a mystery.

A part of the mystery cleared up for him when he got closer and had a look at the side of the car. In large gold lettering it said, "El Paso Electric Railway."

Electric. He'd heard about electric lights. Hadn't ever seen one yet, but he was betting now that he would see one here in the city.

Apparently, this rail coach was electrified somehow.

It didn't seem to hurt anybody, though. There were folks, women in nice dresses and gentlemen in suits and kids in knickers and Mexicans in their white pajamas, riding inside the car, along with two uniformed gents who looked like a proper railroad conductor and engineer, except for them not having a locomotive or caboose or anything attached to this lone car.

No, sir. He couldn't figure what the deal was with this outfit.

But, oh, the wonders to be seen.

Incredible!

Billy was grinning and shaking his head and taking it all in with the excitement of a small boy on Christmas morning.

Yes, sir. El Paso . . . it was *some*.

THIRTEEN

"LORDY, am I ever glad to see *you*," Billy said. His voice reflected weariness. Discouragement. An acute unhappiness that came from simple homesickness.

"Me? What'd I do?"

"Mister, you look like a cowhand. That's what you did."

The skinny man in the wide-brimmed hat grinned and spat a stream of yellow tobacco juice onto the floor of his livery barn. "The city kinda overwhelmin' you, is it, boy?"

"Yes, sir, and then some. I never seen so many folks. And they most all of them look . . . I dunno . . . citified. If you know what I mean."

"Oh, I know, all right. Believe me, I know. Seen it many a time. Felt it my own self when I first come here. There's just s' damn much of it. And all s' busy. Seems hardly healthy."

"That's right. Exactly."

"Look, could be I can help you find your way. What business brought you here?"

"I'm looking for a job of work, mister. No, that isn't exactly right neither. I'm looking to find a career. I got . . . never mind how I come to it for I don't want to seem like I'm whining . . . the thing is, I don't have what I thought I did. And I got a girl to marry and take care of quick as I can get myself established. So I came here . . . mister, l just don't know as I'm cut out for the city life. I mean, there's those railroad cars that run by themselves without a horse nor a locomotive. And all these people. And everybody so busy they don't have time to talk nor even smile. And sir, I got no idea how I can get along. I got practically no money. That never seemed important till now. I have a little food in my poke and a blanket to lay over me at night. But d'you know, a policeman went and ran me off when I tried to lay out my stuff down by the river."

"No, they don't allow that here."

"So I went and talked to a fellow at one of those *ho*-tel places. He said I'd have to pay him a dollar to stay the night and another fifty cents for my horse. For one night."

"Sounds about right," the cowboy said.

"For one night!" Billy repeated. "One."

"Uh-huh."

"And it's too late, well nigh dark now, too late to try and ride back New Mexico way and find a place where I can lay out and get some sleep. And I just didn't know what to do. And then I seen you here, and . . . well, it was sort of like seeing somebody from back home almost."

"Where you from, boy?"

Billy told him.

"I'm down from Montana m'self. Decided t' get away

from the cold for a change, but I don't know yet if I done the right thing." He stuck his hand out. "My name is Monty, by the way. Not really, of course. It's actually Jonathon Theobald. But everybody calls me Monty on account of being from Montana."

"I'm William Delisle. Billy." They shook. "It looks like you're doing well for yourself here, Monty, what with having this place of business."

Monty laughed. "Billy, I've only been here less than a year now, and the business don't belong to me. I work here for wages. The job don't pay much, but it comes with a little room over there with a cot in it an' a stove." He laughed again. "And all the hard corn I care t' eat."

"You're pulling my leg, right?"

"Hell, no, I ain't. What d'you think cornmeal is but ground-up hard corn? I just dip me some out of the grain bin over there an' run it through my coffee grinder. I can make some fine corn dodgers, let me tell you."

"Corn dodgers've always been one of my favorites. My mama used to make them for me."

"Bet mine are ever' bit as good as hers."

"I'd be willing to test that claim, Monty, and give you an opinion about it."

"Then I expect I'll have to make you some. Tell you what, Billy. The boss don't come around much, an' he never told me I couldn't have a guest in. I'm honor-bound to collect a quarter for your horse . . . should be fifty cents, you understand, but there's a commercial discount for regular customers, so I'm not cheating him none if I only collect the quarter off you. And you can lay your stuff out on the floor in my room there. No charge for that. Or sleep up in the loft if you'd rather that." He grinned. "I been told that I snore pretty bad, though I can't say as I necessarily believe it, havin' never heard myself snore, if you see what I mean."

"I can pay you . . . ." Billy dug in his pockets. "I got twenty cents. Can you cut it to that?"

Monty pulled at his chin, then shook his head. "No, I expect that wouldn't be right. I can't cheat the boss like that."

Billy's expression sagged. "I understand. Right is right and wrong is wrong. I wouldn't ask you to go against your own boss."

"No, I won't do that. But what I will do, Billy, is I'll hire you t' do the morning feeding t'morrow. The job ain't much. Only pays twenty-five cents. Think you'd be interested in a preposition like that?"

Billy did not correct the gentleman's grammar. What he did do was to grin. "I accept," he said quick before Monty could take it back.

FOURTEEN

BILLY used the tines of a pitchfork to drag a heap of hay—it was a little too dry in his opinion, but there was no mold on it and didn't seem too bad—over to the edge of the trapdoor opening. He could hear voices in the barn, Monty and a customer, he assumed.

"Look out below." He waited a couple seconds and when no one hollered to object, he kicked the hay into the opening and let it fall. It would have been easier and more efficient to throw the hay out the loft window into the feed-lot at the back of the barn, but if he did that, the horses and mules in the corral would rush into it and ruin too much by trampling on it. It was better to take it down this way and then carry it out to the feed bunk a forkful at a time.

He leaned the big fork up against one of the roof supports ready for the next time, then climbed down the ladder and took up the downstairs pitchfork.

Over by the front door, Monty was talking with a tall, cadaverously lean gent wearing a black cutaway suit coat, red silk vest, and a derby hat that had seen better days. The man had a huge mustache, black as black could get and big enough to fill a quart pail, Billy figured, if you shaved it off him and tried to pack it. His hair was liberally flecked with gray and needed cutting about as bad as his hat needed cleaning.

He looked . . . Billy couldn't quite decide . . . like a small-time gambler. Or maybe a traveling salesman for ladies' clothing. He also had a thin, rather nasal voice.

Billy scooped a hefty load of hay onto the fork, and carried it out into the feedlot to the bunk. The animals were already gathered close around it, and he had to push his way in between a mule's scrawny butt and that of a brown horse in order to reach the feeder. He deposited that load and went back for another.

Half an hour later, when he was done filling the hay bunk and had grained the indoor horses, whose owners paid extra to have them put up in a stall and fed better than the plain grass hay, he went to join Monty in the hostler's room. There was an aroma of corn dodgers in the air, and Billy's mouth was running fit to overflow the banks of a good-sized creek.

"All done with the feeding?"

Billy nodded.

"You gave an extry scoop o' mixed grain to that damned snake-neck blue horse, did you?"

"Just like you told me to."

Monty grunted. The blue roan was a high-stepping buggy horse for the banker's mistress. Not that there was anything wrong with that, but the damn thing was a kicker and a biter and seemed to hate male human persons. Or so Monty claimed. He hadn't given Billy any trouble.

When Billy mentioned that, Monty grunted. "O' course he wouldn't. Not right off. He's a sneaky sumbish. First, he lulls you to sleep. Next thing, you're trusting him and he'll try and bite a chunk outa your back. Just you wait an' see."

"I'll keep an eye on him. Say, when are those pones gonna be ready?"

"Couple more minutes. Set down. I won't let you starve."

Billy grinned. And sat.

"Say, d'you remember that fella was here when you come down from the loft?"

"Sure."

Monty grinned. "Recognize him?"

"No, should I?"

"Not if you don't pay attention to that sort o' stuff, I suppose."

"What stuff?"

"Ever hear of a gent named Tucker Adler?"

"Of course, but . . ." Billy's eyes went wide. "Him? That was Tuck Adler? In person?"

"One and the same," Monty said, sounding as proud as if he'd personally invented the man.

"Lordy. Oh, Lordy. Imagine that. I've read all his books. I mean . . . you know . . . the books about him."

Tucker Adler, the gentleman gunfighter, was almost as famous as Wild Bill Hickok or the Earp Brothers or Buffalo Bill Cody, Texas Jack Omohundro, Clay Allison, John Wesley Hardin . . . any of them. Thrilling stories were written about him, just like about those other gunmen of the old-time Wild West.

"That was really him? Honest?"

"Honest and true," Monty said. "The big bay in that corner stall is his. This morning he was checking to see if it's healed proper from a stone bruise it got a while back. Said he might need t' be doing some riding soon."

"Wow. I wonder where. Is he after some outlaws, do you think?"

Monty shrugged. "I dunno, but a man like Tuck Adler . . . could be. Most anything's possible. You know about those times do you, Billy?"

"Oh my, yes. I've read about them all."

"Did you know it's not more'n a mile to the place where John Wesley Hardin was shot down and killed?"

"I never . . . it was in El Paso, wasn't it?"

"Yep. Not quite ten years ago, that was. I'll take you over there and show you the place later on. I got a carriage to hitch and deliver over near there anyhow. You can come with me and see. They got a bronze plate on the floor to mark the exact spot where he breathed his last. That Hardin, they say he was something of a gent too. I never met him myself, but most folks here who knew him liked him well enough. That's what they say now anyhow."

"Tuck Adler, though . . ." Billy's eyes went wide again. "That hat. You don't think . . . ?"

"Yep. One an' the same," Monty assured him.

Adler's fame began back in . . . Billy couldn't remember for sure now . . . the late 1870's maybe or early '80's. They said Adler was clerking in a dry-goods store in Kansas at the time. After work one evening, he got into what was supposed to be a friendly card game. He said later that he caught the tinhorn dealer cheating. Hot words followed, and Adler was braced by the gambler and two of his pals.

The gambler, whose name was forgotten to history, threw down on Adler with a sleeve gun and both his cronies went for their .45's.

Tuck Adler, incredibly, got the first shots off. He drilled the gambler square in the chest, and killed both the other two as well using a pair of six-guns that he wore out of sight in shoulder holsters.

Adler was not hit in the exchange, but his wide-brimmed Stetson was ruined by a bullet fired by one of the opponents. It was said that Adler coolly tossed his Stetson into the blood on the still-warm corpse of the gambler and appropriated the tinhorn's fancy derby hat to replace it.

"Wow. The hat and everything. I didn't know he lived here."

"He didn't," Monty said. "Not until lately. He showed up here, oh, a little better than a week ago maybe. I don't know where he come from nor where he's going. Just know he pays his bill, and that's something I can't say about just everybody."

"Wow," Billy said again.

"So tell me. D'you want to keep on jawing, or would you like to see how these corn dodgers stack up?"

Billy grinned. "Bring on those dodgers."

"Comin' right up," Monty said as he reached for the lid of the Dutch oven.

FIFTEEN

THE strange-looking rail cars that ran without an engine were indeed electrified. They were called streetcars, and the electric to power them was carried in the cables above the street. The long, whippy rod things on the roofs were actually gadgets that picked up the electric off the cable and took it somehow down to whatever sort of motor— mighty powerful motor too—that drove them.

Billy actually got to ride in one of the contraptions.

Monty had to deliver three hundredweight of grain to a fire station, and then take the wagon along to a storekeeper who wanted to rent the rig, and he took Billy with him. They rode a streetcar to get back to the livery.

Oh, it was something, it was. The car jolted and jounced some, although not so bad as an unsprung farm wagon, and it took off with a lurch, as there didn't seem to be all that much choice of speed for the engineer to make. Either the streetcar was stopped or it was moving.

"I'll tell you what they always remind me of," Monty said. "Dang sand beetles, the way they scurry along paying no mind to anything on either side." He snorted. "That reminds me. You shoulda been here a couple weeks ago. Now that was excitement, I'm telling you.

"Fella in one of those horseless automobiles ran into one of the streetcars. Smashed his gasoline contraption pretty bad and led to some real serious cussing, I can tell you."

"Was anybody hurt?"

"Naw. Couple ladies got their hats knocked off when the streetcar stopped so sudden, but that was about it. The fella steering the automobile said he got his wheel stuck inside a rail and couldn't swerve outa the way quick enough. Now mind you, he's the one run into the streetcar, which for sure couldn't move outa the way, yet he got mad at the streetcar conductor for not avoiding him." Monty shook his head. "Some folks can't see themselves if you put them in a room full o' mirrors."

"I wish I'd seen that."

"Yeah, it was something, all right. Wait a second. We'll get off at this next corner."

They were not back where they started near the livery, but Billy followed Monty down the steps to the street—he pretty much had to stick on Monty like a burr on a sock because he wasn't sure he could find his way back to the barn on his own—and into a hotel on a busy street corner.

It was actually a small saloon in the downstairs of the hotel. Which must have been four, maybe five stories tall. And at that wasn't even the tallest structure in El Paso. The bar was right at the corner of the building and a person could enter right from the street.

"See that spot over there?"

Billy nodded.

"That's the place. That right there."

"That's where Hardin was shot down?"

"The very spot."

"Wow."

"Want a beer?" Monty offered.

"No, thanks."

"Want something harder?"

Billy shook his head. "I haven't ever got around to taking up drinking."

"Beer isn't bad. It's good for the stomach, y'know. And if you buy one, you can tackle the free lunch along with it. Sure you don't want to change your mind?"

The ham and pickled eggs set at the end of the bar—not but a few feet away from where the notorious gunman died—did look pretty good.

"Maybe a small one then."

Monty chuckled and led the way to the bar, while Billy sidled over close to the free lunch layout.

The beer, served in a mug of exceptionally thick and heavy glass so that it looked bigger on the outside than it actually was on the inside, proved to have a sharp, slightly bitter taste that Billy didn't much care for.

"Will this make me drunk?"

"If you drink enough of it, sure 't will."

"I wonder what my mama and the folks back at our church meeting would say if they could see me with this in my hand and beer on my breath."

"If they're straitlaced and hidebound, they'd prob'ly

say you was going straight to Hell. D'you feel any different, like the devil's of a sudden got into you?"

"No," Billy admitted. "I expect that I don't."

"To my mind anyhow, there's a world o' difference between being drunk an' having a beer or even two."

"I'll have to think on that some."

"Hand me another egg there, would you?"

Nope, he wasn't all that fond of the beer. But there wasn't a thing in the world wrong with the lunch that came with it. He gave Monty the requested egg, and used the tongs to fish out a couple more for himself while he was at it.

SIXTEEN

MONTY was a heckuva nice fellow, and Billy was glad to have encountered him. No, not glad. Make that grateful instead. But the fact was, nice though Monty was, Billy could not go on living at Monty's expense. He needed a job.

Not only did he need "a" job, he needed a darned good job. He needed a job not for his own comfort—he didn't need hardly anything—but he needed one good enough that he could support Edie as his wife. That right there was the important thing. Billy would take on anything, anything at all, if it would enable him to marry Edie.

He was offered jobs during his all-day every-day searching. Most of them, unfortunately, were on the order of becoming a saloon swamper, emptying spittoons and sweeping floors. Heck, he would gladly have done that for a permanent career if it meant having Edie here. But the pay for a job like that would run to a couple dollars cash money each week and two glasses of bar whiskey a day. Not exactly something a man could take a wife on.

He was offered one job driving a phaeton for a snooty rich woman. That one sounded promising, until he found out in a downright embarrassing way that what she wanted wasn't so much a driver as a . . . well . . . not just a driver. That one *sure* wasn't a job for a married man.

He kept looking. But after several days he was becoming discouraged. He went back to the livery with a heavy heart. He had exactly ten cents remaining in his pockets, and he spent that to buy crackers and cheese so he would be able to contribute at least a little bit to Monty's larder.

"You look mighty down in the mouth this evenin'. Still no job?"

Billy shook his head.

"How would you like a nice, steady government job that pays seventy-five a month?"

"Oh, that'd be fine," Billy said, "but all the good jobs take skills that I don't have. Believe me, I'm finding out about that lately."

"Then how would you like a nice government job like I just said if the skill needed was t' be able to ride a horse."

"Don't be twisting my leg, Monty. I'm not in the mood for it right now."

"Hey, I'm serious. What would you think about something like that?"

"Monty, I'd kill for a job like that."

The Montana cowboy pulled at his chin and stuck his lip out. He shook his head and said, "I doubt it would come to that. But I s'pose you never know."

"Monty, what the devil are you talking about?"

"You remember Tuck Adler."

"Of course I remember Tuck Adler. Everybody remembers Tuck Adler."

"Right. Well, he was in here again today, and he was telling me about this new government outfit . . . Federal, not the city or the state, mind, but the Federal government . . . and all that's needed is to ride along the border and turn back anybody that isn't s'posed to be crossing into the U.S. of A."

"You're kidding me, right?"

"Nope. I'm telling you the natural truth just exactly like he told to me. I expect he thought I might be interested. Truth is, I'm not. I kinda like the deal I got here and don't want to leave it. But this sounds like it could be just the right thing for you."

"Where do I . . . ?"

Monty pulled a slip of paper from his pocket. "I got the information writ down for you right here. Even got the name of the man you're to see. And you can tell him . . . I checked this to make absolutely sure . . . you can tell this man that Tuck Adler recommended you for the job."

"He knows. . . ."

"He saw you here the other day. Remembered when I mentioned you to him. He said you looked likely and you could use his name. Oh, I forgot. There's one other requirement for the job, one that keeps most young men around here from qualifying for the position."

"Monty, you already know I don't have much in the way of skills to offer. As a cowboy I'm not even very good with a rope."

Monty grinned. "This other job requirement, Billy. It's that the candidate has to have his own horse. The government isn't supplying those. Has to have a horse and a bedroll and be willing to ride for long hours."

"Lord knows I can do that."

"Adler said the man will be in his office by eight-thirty tomorrow morning."

"And I'll be waiting outside his door when he shows up," Billy said.

"How's about some of my world-famous, better'n-your-mama's corn dodgers to celebrate."

"I don't have the job yet. And I've never once told you that your dodgers are better than my mama's. But if you want to make them, I expect I'd do my part by eating them for you."

Of a sudden, all the burdens he'd been carrying sloughed clean off his back, and Billy felt lighter than air.

Seventy-five dollars each and every month? He could support a wife in fine style on that much money.

Yes!

SEVENTEEN

BILLY was feeling more than a little self-conscious. Both the other fellows who were waiting to see Major Bolton and the man who'd just gone inside were all neatly dressed in suits and collars and neckties, while all he had were his old jeans and a shirt he'd scrubbed more or less clean in the horse trough. He'd polished his boots with some colored wax Monty loaned him, and that was about the best he had been able to manage this morning. He felt like a brown rooster in a room full of peacocks.

The major's door opened and the fellow who'd gone in ahead of Billy emerged. He was a man who looked to be about in his middle thirties, tall and muscular and well set-up. He looked satisfied, and Billy hoped the job wasn't filled up yet.

A bald little fellow appeared in the open doorway. He

tipped his chin down so he could peer over the top of a pair of Ben Franklin half-spectacles. "Who's next out here?"

One of the college boys on the far side of the room— Billy didn't actually know that's what they were, but they looked like they ought to be—nodded in Billy's direction, acknowledging that he was next in line.

With a flutter in his belly, for never in his life had he ever done anything remotely like this, he stood and went through the door that the little fellow held open for him.

"Excuse me. Where is Major Bolton?"

The little man scowled. "I am he. Were you expecting someone else?"

"No, sir, I thought . . . ." Billy shut his mouth before he got himself in any deeper. He wasn't about to admit that he'd taken the major who was in charge of this shebang for an office clerk.

Bolton smiled a little, and Billy guessed that the little man knew good and well what Billy'd thought. "Over here. Sit down. Let's start with your name, shall we?"

There was a large desk with a swivel chair behind it, and an armchair placed in front of it for the job applicants. Orderly piles of printed forms lay on the desk, along with an assortment of pens and stamps and blotters and the biggest inkwell Billy ever saw. Along the front there were trays where more papers were filed.

Billy introduced himself, adding he was there at the recommendation of Mr. Adler.

"You say Tucker sent you?"

"More or less, sir. He told my friend about the job and said that I ought to apply too. But I expect it was my friend who brought it up seeing as how I'm looking for work and he isn't. I can't claim that I really know Mr. Adler. He keeps his horse at the stable where I've been staying with this friend."

Bolton jotted something down on one of his forms. Billy wished he could see what he was writing there. Or come to think of it, maybe he was better off not seeing.

"Are you aware that this position requires you to provide your own horse?"

"Yes, sir. Mr. Adler told my friend that."

"Do you own a horse?"

"Yes, sir."

"Did you ride him here today?"

"No, sir."

"How old is this horse?"

It seemed an odd question, but Billy said, "Seven. If I remember correct, that is. I think he's seven coming eight."

"What color?"

"Sir? The color of my horse? Does that make a difference?"

"In a manner of speaking, yes. Can you answer the question?"

"He's gray, sir. A gelding. Not too big, just a hair over fifteen hands. He's a good cow horse and an easy traveler."

"Hmm. You really do have a horse, I take it."

"I already told you that, sir."

"Most of the young men I see are willing to buy a horse if they get this job, Mr. Delisle, but they do not already own one. For some reason, many seem to think they have to lie and claim to already own one. If there is one thing I cannot abide, it is dishonesty. I would not at all mind a man telling me that he will buy a mount if he needs one, but those who lie to me about it are instantly disqualified."

"I see, sir. I expect it makes sense to me now. Thank you."

"Are you twenty-one?"

"Yes, sir, I am."

"And a citizen of the United States?"

"Yes, sir. Born in New Mexico Territory. Lived there all my life until recent."

"Can you read and write?"

"Yes, sir."

"Know right from wrong?"

"I was brought up to know the difference, yes, sir."

Bolton sat back in his chair and folded his arms over his chest. He sat there silently peering at Billy for what seemed a very long time, although it probably was not more than a minute or so. Billy waited patiently for him to go on with the interview.

"My men operate alone or in very small groups. They may be away from headquarters here for months at a time operating on their own initiative with little or no input from higher authority. The border we patrol extends down the Rio Grande to the Gulf of Mexico and westward across country to the Pacific Ocean. I have been authorized to hire up to seventy-five men to patrol this rather large area of responsibility. Are you afraid of hard work, Mr. Delisle?"

"No, sir. And if it matters, I'm used to being on my own, chasing cows outa the brush and like that."

"Our primary responsibility is to turn back would-be illegal immigrants. Chinese, for the most part. Do you think you can handle that?"

"Well, sir, I expect I can recognize a Chinaman when I see one. But I got to tell you straight out I'm not all that good with a rope. I hope the job doesn't include roping and hog-tying them." He smiled. "Nor branding them neither, though I'm better with a branding iron than with the rope."

Bolton laughed. "Up until now I've hired twenty-six men to become Chinese Immigration Agents. Or Mounted Inspectors if you prefer to call yourself that. You will be number twenty-seven. Please keep that number in mind. Your official reports, expense vouchers, and so on will all be filed under the serial number zero-two-seven."

"Sir, do you mean . . . ?"

"You have the job, Mr. Delisle. Agent Delisle, I should say now. You're hired."

Billy grinned.

Bolton wrote something on a slip of paper and pushed it across the desk. "Report to this address tomorrow at seven o'clock sharp. You will be given an orientation talk and an assignment."

Billy was still grinning when he left the little major's office.

EIGHTEEN

AFTER spending half the morning being lectured to by a man named Thomas—whether that was his first name or last was never made quite clear—Billy reported back to Major Bolton, who swore him in and handed him a badge.

Billy peered at the surprisingly heavy burnished steel object in his hand. "I didn't expect. . . ."

"You are a law-enforcement agent now," the major said. He added a thin smile. "Well, more or less."

"Why does it say Special Deputy on it?"

The smile grew larger. "Because there's no such thing yet as a Chinese Immigration Agent badge."

"I reckon that's just as well. I think I prefer Mounted Inspector anyway."

"Did Thomas give you your assignment yet?"

"Yes, sir. He said I'm to go with a fellow named Nate

Williams and drift west through New Mexico and Arizona and see what we see over that way."

"If you have no objection, Agent Delisle, I am going to change that assignment. Agent Adler has asked that you be his partner. Would that be acceptable to you?"

"Sir?" Billy was beyond surprised. He was flabbergasted. Tuck Adler wanted him for a partner? Billy wondered if Monty were for some reason responsible for the request.

Why? He shook his head. It didn't matter why. It was fantastic. Marvelous. A genuinely famous man like Tucker Adler wanted *him* for a partner. Incredible.

"Do I take it that you would rather not ride with Agent Adler then?" the major asked.

It took Billy a moment to realize why he'd said that. "Oh. No. I was . . . I was shaking my head about something else, sir. I'd be honored to ride with a man like Mr. . . . I mean, Agent Adler. If you think I'm up to it."

"I am quite certain you are up to the task, Agent Delisle. All I ask from you is an honest effort."

"I can give you that, sir. I surely can."

"I believe you, son." The major extended his hand, and Mounted Inspector Billy Delisle shook it.

NINETEEN

"WELL, I'm ready to go."

The gentleman gunfighter peered at him across the back of his leggy bay horse. He took several long moments, more than long enough to make Billy feel uncomfortable with the scrutiny. "Go where?"

"Why . . . on patrol. Wherever you say."

Tuck Adler's brows knitted in deep concentration. Then comprehension quite obviously came to him. "You're the kid who's riding with me, right?"

Billy was crestfallen. Adler hadn't even recognized him. The man asked to partner with him, but did not even recognize him now. Not that there was anything Billy could actually say. But his disappointment was acute. "Yes, sir. I'm Billy Delisle."

Adler grunted and said, "All right then. You know who I am. But let me get something straight here. You don't go

calling me 'sir.' Makes me feel old. You can call me Tuck.
You can call me Adler. You can call me that rotten
sonuvabitch if you think you're man enough. But don't go
calling me 'sir.' "

"Yes, s . . . Mr. Adler. I'll try and remember that."

"See that you do. Now . . . you were saying something
about being ready to go?"

"Yes, s . . . Mr. Adler."

"Well, I'm not ready to go. There's some things I got to
do first. I expect I'll be back in two, three days. We'll head
down the river then. Take the train east to San Angelo,
maybe San Antone, then strike south on the old highway
through Dogtown . . . or whatever the hell they've gone
and named it now . . . to Laredo. I figure you and me will
patrol up and down the river with Laredo as our base. I already told the major that and it's fine with him. All you got
to do is what I tell you, all right?"

"Yes, sir."

"What'd I tell you about that?"

"Oh. Sorry. I'll get it straight. It just might take me a
while."

"All right." He frowned and looked Billy over again.
"Where's your gun, boy? You said you're ready to go, and
I see your stuff rolled on that horse, and you got no gun on
your belt nor anyplace else that I can see. Get it outa that
bedroll and strap it on. Gun won't do you no damn good if
it's kept away where you can't lay hands on it."

"I don't own a gun, s . . . Mr. Adler. The major never
said anything about me having to have one."

"He might not 've, but I'm telling you. You got to have
you a gun. Get one before I get back here."

"Yes, sir, but . . . I'm broke."

Adler rolled his eyes and swore. "Here." He dug into a pocket and handed Billy a twenty-dollar gold piece. "You can pay me back come payday. Just make sure you're wearing a gun when I get back here."

"Yes, s . . . Mr. Adler. What am I supposed to do while you're away? I can't just sit around the barn here drawing pay and not doing anything for it."

"Go over to the Juarez side and look around. See if there's any concentrations of Chinamen we need to be looking out for. If you see any, you needn't do anything about it right then, but you can report back to me when I get here and I'll see if I think anything needs to be done with them. All right?"

"Yes, s . . . Mr. Adler. I'll do just what you say."

Adler grunted again and swung onto the bay horse. "I'll be back in two, three days. Wait for me."

"Yes, sir."

Adler let that slip of his tongue slide by without comment, reining the bay toward the street and quickly out of sight.

Billy stood there for a moment looking after his partner agent and then down at the coin that lay bright in his hand. He shook his head. This was not exactly the introduction to Mounted Inspector work that he'd envisioned.

Not that it was his place to question Mr. Adler.

Billy slipped the double eagle into his pocket and went to see where Monty was. He could use some advice since he knew practically nothing about firearms.

TWENTY

THIS was exciting. Billy didn't know all that much about firearms, but for as long as he could remember he had read everything he could find concerning the old Wild West days and the scouts and Indian fighters and famous gunfighters.

And now he was going to be riding partners with one of the most famous gunfighters of them all.

Even wearing a badge and carrying a gun.

Once he bought one.

The place Monty directed him to was not a gunsmith's, though, nor a hardware, but a pawnshop located not far from the upstream one of the two bridges across to the Juarez side of the Rio Grande. The shop was on a side street, and over the door instead of a regular sign, it had three metal balls hanging from one iron bar like three grapes on a single stem.

"Can I help you?" The proprietor was a small man with thinning hair and a small mustache.

Billy explained his mission and added, "Monty over at the livery stable sent me. He said I should tell you I'm a friend of his."

The proprietor smiled. "Monty worries too much. Everyone is treated fair here. But it is good of him to take care of your interests. He also takes care of mine, you see, whenever I need to rent a buggy or a wagon. I will make sure to give you a very good deal. Do you know what you want?"

"No, sir. I don't know guns all that well."

"What a refreshing change. Everyone else who comes here to look for a gun believes he knows everything about them."

"I'd sure be lying to claim that."

"So are they. But most do not know that themselves. Let me show you what I have, eh?" He used a small key taken from his watch pocket to unlock the glass-front display case, and pulled out several heavy trays laden with revolvers and derringers and even one ancient cap-lock pepperbox. "So. You are looking for a gun to carry in the pocket for personal defense? Something to hide in your sleeve? Something to impress the young ladies and show you are a tough hombre? Something to pot at rabbits with or turn an angry cow?"

"Something to wear on my belt to go with a badge," Billy said.

"A badge, is it? Funny, you do not look like a policeman."

Billy explained.

"This I have never heard of. Will you have to shoot at people? People will shoot at you?"

"Lord, I hope not. But my partner says I got to have a gun, so I expect I'd best be getting one."

The man picked up a Colt six-shooter like Billy had seen around home pretty much his whole life long. "This is the popular revolver here. Fairly durable. Fairly accurate. Fairly expensive because they are so popular, you see."

"Yes, sir, I've seen those before."

"These little guns here, you do not want one of them. Too small. They are fine to carry, but most are not well made and they are not so accurate. Besides, if you ever do have to shoot somebody, God forbid, you might hit them and make them mad. These guns, they are better for the making of noise to frighten away burglars.

"Now this"—he held up a rather large revolver—"this one you should look at. This one I recommend to you."

"Why's that?"

"This one is a Smith and Wesson double-action .44-caliber revolver. It is more accurate than the Colt there and more rugged. It will last you a long time. Much quicker to reload too. Look." He tripped a catch near the hammer and tilted the barrel down. The whole barrel and cylinder opened up and a little hand-like pawl flipped up, then withdrew again into the back end of the cylinder.

"See there? I will show you again. See it? That little whatchamacallit, it throws the spent cartridge casings out. You drop fresh cartridges into the chambers. Close it like this. You are ready to shoot again. If you are in a hurry, you only have to pull on the trigger. Like so. The cylinder rotates and the hammer pulls back and drops to fire the gun.

If you want best accuracy and to aim, you cock the gun . . . like so . . . and it fires just like the single action. Double action, that means it will work from just pulling the trigger. Like this. Do you see?"

Billy nodded.

"The Colts, they are pretty. They are very good guns. But you have to cock them every time before you shoot. And they are not so rugged as this one. This one"—he shrugged—"not so pretty. But a very good gun.

"Now we get to the biggest difference, eh? This Colt here, average condition, probably twenty, thirty years old. Might need a mainspring soon depending on the last time that was replaced. Because these are so popular, this Colt, it is costing you sixteen dollars. Twice that if you want to buy a new one.

"This .44 Smith and Wesson that I recommend to you, not so popular, only eight or ten years old probably, it is costing you six dollars. Normally eight, but that Monty would be mad with me and give me a flighty horse if I fail to make a good deal. So, for you, six dollars only."

Billy took the Smith from the man. It was heavier than it looked. But also more comfortable in the hand than he expected from just looking at it. He fumbled with the catch and opened the mechanism, and the little hand popped up and then went down again. He sighted along the barrel and pulled the trigger, then tried it again after cocking the hammer first. The pull was much harder if he did not cock it first.

"I'll take it," he said.

"This Smith and Wesson then?"

"Yes, sir."

"You will want cartridges, I think. No good having a

MAN ON THE BORDER 75

gun if you do not have the cartridges. Enough so you can practice with it. You should learn to shoot it. And you will need a holster. I have some in a box here. Pick through these and find one you like."

The pawnshop owner got his eight dollars after all.

Billy had the man wrap his purchases in brown butcher paper tied with string. He would have felt silly wearing a gun in town. Especially one he had never shot and for all practical purposes did not yet know how to shoot.

Walking back to the livery with a gun, his own gun, he felt . . . different somehow. Taller. Stronger. More grown-up.

But then after all, he was employed now as a law officer—well, sort of—and he had a badge and a gun. He supposed he really ought to feel strong and capable and all grown-up.

He whistled a little as he returned to the livery to show Monty what he'd bought.

TWENTY-ONE

TUCK Adler was gone for five days. When he returned, he gave no explanation about where he had been or why.

By that time Billy had become almost frantic with worry and indecision. How long should he wait before he went to Major Bolton and asked for instructions? The major thought his new agents were somewhere south along the border by now diligently finding illegal Chinese and turning them back.

Billy did not want his first act as a Mounted Inspector to consist of peaching on his own partner. Nor did he want to get fired himself, which he had to believe was possible if the major decided he and Mr. Adler were just dogging it while drawing the government's pay.

He spent the time either over on the Mexican side—where the sights were interesting but entirely devoid of Chinese as far as he could tell—or along the riverbank practicing with his new revolver. After shooting up another six dollars worth of ammunition, Billy proved himself a more than competent shot when it came to accuracy. At any reasonable distance, the big Smith shot within fractions of an inch of his point of aim.

He had also determined that he was not and likely never would be very quick to bring his gun into action. Men like Adler and Hickok, Earp and Masterson, Allison and Hardin might well go into action in a flash just like all those luridly exciting books said. Ordinary mortals like Billy Delisle could only grab and yank as best they were able.

Which was entirely all right with Billy really. Gunfighting pretty much necessitated that someone be hurt. He did not want to hurt another soul on earth. Not even Leon Soames, damn the man.

When he was done practicing with the revolver, Billy would hop onto a streetcar—the cars were a continual source of amazement and delight no matter how many times he rode them—and go across the river to explore on the Juarez side just like he'd been instructed to do.

He found no Chinese, but he did spot a beautiful pair of spurs with large rowels, silver jinglers, and thin chains to go under the instep and hold them down. The third time he came back to admire them, the proprietor of the tiny shop made him such a deal that Billy simply could not resist any longer. He'd never in his life owned such a splendid article, and felt pretty grand now walking around with the .44 Smith on his hip and those silver jinglers making music with every step he took.

None of that was what he was being paid to do, however, and it was with great relief that he finally saw Adler and the tall bay horse coming up the street in the soft light of early evening.

"I see you're heeled, boy. That's good." Adler stepped off the bay and handed Billy the reins. "Take care of him for me, would you? Be ready at first light. We're leaving first thing in the morning."

With that, Agent Adler was gone again.

Billy looked at the horse, which showed no signs of hard use during the past few days, and in fact looked fat and glossy with no dust marring its splendid coat, then shrugged and went to work to pull Adler's saddle and give the horse a rubdown and feeding. It was either that or Monty would have to take care of it, and Billy did not want to become a burden on a man who had so befriended him.

Leaving in the morning, were they? Fine. Tonight, he decided, he would treat Monty Theobald to a steak dinner. He had enough money left over for that even after he stocked up on a little grub to tuck away in his bedroll.

That was it for sure, he thought with pleasure. He would stand treat for Monty and him to have a grand blowout on his last night in El Paso.

And tomorrow he would start earning his keep as a Mounted Inspector.

TWENTY-TWO

Dearest Mr. Delisle:

It was with great interest, may I be so bold as to say anticipation, that I rec'd yrs of 11th inst concerning your employment opportunity.

Papa was impressed to find you doing so very good so soon, but I think he is worried that you will do too good too soon. Papa and Mama are not ready to think of me as a grown woman. I am confident they will give their consent when you return to do what you said you will do. If you still have that intention, as you did not mention in our last. Do you?

Billy, I must tell you that I worry about you now that you are an officer of the Law. It is my ernest desire that you keep yourself secure and above harm so that you may return here at the earliest.

My prayers will continue for you, which they do

each night, and will redouble in light of this new and dangerous circumstance.

I expect to see your mama this Sabbath forenoon. I will inform her of your wellbeing, but in accord with your wishes will not explain further.

Please know, my dearest, that my fondness for you is unbounded and undying. I await your return and pray for you constantly until that time shall come.

Yrs in affection,

Edith Jane Forester

Dear Miss Forester,

I take pen in hand while traveling in a rail car inroute to San Antonio, Tex, where my partner tells me we shall debark and take horse for a town of his intimate acquaintance called Marley, on the river somewhere north of Laredo, southeast from Del Rio.

Please do not worry about my safety. My duties are not of a dangerous nature. Where formerly I herded beeves, now I shall herd people, rounding up illegal immigrants and herding them back across the border where they belong, or if it becomes necessary, even taking them under guard to San Francisco for deportation back to China. I rather hope I will have that opportunity to see San Francisco. Someday I would like to be able to show it to you.

Do I make you blush? That is not my intention. My desire is only to reassure you that you remain constantly in my thoughts and that my only desire is to once again have the pleasure of your presence.

Please convey my regards and good wishes to your father, your mother, and to Jason also.

Please do not worry yourself on my account as I am in good health and excellent spirits and look forward to once more casting my eyes upon your countenance.

With deepest affection,
William Delisle

He'd struggled with the letter, particularly the decision about whether he should mention the name of his famous partner. In the end he had decided against that. Mr. Forester was certain to know Mr. Adler's name, and the knowledge would only make Edie worry all the more.

Billy blotted his signature and capped the ink bottle. The scenes flickering past the window of the passenger coach went unnoticed. All he could see before him was Edie's face.

Soon, he promised himself. Soon.

TWENTY-THREE

MR. Adler led the way back along the train to the stock car, where the horses had made the trip. Four sweating, smiling Negroes muscled a portable ramp up to the side of the car, and slid the door open so Adler and Billy and one other traveler could off-load their horses.

The other man led his off afoot. Adler and Billy saddled and mounted.

"Will we be looking around the city some before we leave?"

"Why?" Adler asked. "You want a woman before we go?"

Billy felt his ears commence to turn warm, but he was determined not to let that sort of thing bother him. After all, this was a famous man. And he was in charge of where they went and what they did. Billy didn't figure it was his business to complain or make any demands on Tucker

Adler. "No. I just thought . . . well . . . since we're right here . . . I'd kinda like to see the Alamo. Lord knows I've heard enough about it all my life."

Adler grunted. "Don't say I didn't warn you if you're disappointed then."

"We can see it?"

"We'll go by there on our way outa town."

Billy grinned.

Half an hour later the grin was gone. The fabled Alamo wasn't anything more than an old adobe mission church slowly melting into the ground. It didn't look at all like he'd expected it to. He'd thought it was large and imposing. It was small and dreary and trash littered the ground around it.

"Is it what you thought to see here?" Adler asked him.

"No, sir." The older man forgot for once to get after him for calling him "sir." "I reckon it isn't." He stood in his stirrups and craned his neck around. "For one thing, in all the stuff I've read about this place, nobody ever mentioned the river running right past."

"Hell, it ain't much of a river. Not worth the mention." Adler turned his head and spat.

Indeed, the San Antonio was about as poor and scruffy a river as the Alamo was a shrine to freedom. Its banks were trash-strewn and brush-choked, and its course was sunken a good twenty feet or more below street level.

"Tie your horse over there, kid." Adler dismounted.

"Where're we going?"

"In there." Adler jerked a thumb in the direction of the Alamo. Billy followed him into the shadowy interior. Spears of sunlight caught dust motes swirling in the air.

Most of the roof had collapsed, letting in light and air and rain too, which no doubt contributed to the mess inside.

"Take your hat off, boy. This might be a tumbledown old sonuvabitch, but it's still a church, you know."

Billy snatched his hat off and stood in the middle of a large room where less than seventy-five years ago Crockett and Travis and all those others had stood and fought and died. The thought gave him a chill, and of a sudden this no longer was a crappy, falling-down old building. It really was a shrine. It really was a place of deep and special feeling, and he sensed that he would not look at it again and be disappointed.

Adler squinted at him, and apparently saw the reverence registered on Billy's face. "Is this more like what you expected?"

"Yes, sir. It surely is."

"Come on then. We got miles to make."

Outside, Tuck Adler removed his coat and carefully folded it and tied it behind his cantle. They mounted, and Adler led the way down to a well-traveled highway, macadamed for the first mile or so, and then reverting to the usual dust and caliche ruts.

"This road goes to Laredo, but we won't follow it that long. We'll go down about to Tilden, then turn off to the west."

"Yes, sir."

"I thought I told you already not to call me that." Adler snapped at him.

"Yes, s . . . Mr. Adler."

TWENTY-FOUR

BILLY had assumed that the Gentleman Gunfighter would want to travel fancy, putting up at hotels or wayside inns along the way. Instead, come late afternoon, Adler reined away from the road and into someone's fenced pasture.

"There'll be a stock tank underneath that windmill over there," Adler said. "We'll lay out beside it for the night."

Billy hadn't even noticed the telltale Aeromotor vanes peeking up above a small, brushy motte of mixed wood and feathery mesquite.

The older man eyed Billy closely as he unsaddled his horse and tugged the cord to turn the windmill on. The inevitable stock tank was there, but was not full. Likely there were no beeves in this particular trap at the moment, so there was no need for the pump to draw. Thirty feet or so overhead, the tail of the windmill was swiveled about by a slight evening breeze. The big fan groaned into position facing the flow of air, and began to revolve, slowly at first and then with gathering authority. Soon, a thin trickle of water began to flow from the pipe, spilling into the huge galvanized tank.

Billy unsaddled his gray and rubbed it down, then hobbled it and turned it loose to drink and pick at the lush grass that grew in the shade close by the windmill. "You keep looking at me. Is something wrong?"

"Nope. Just wondering when you're going to ask me about should we go get permission to camp here."

"Mr. Adler, I may be mighty green when it comes to lawing and man-chasing and all like that. But I was raised on a ranch in the south of New Mexico Territory. I expect I know what's trespass in country like this and what isn't."

Adler grunted and gave him a look that Billy thought just might possibly be reappraisal. In a very small way, that is.

"Fetch us some wood, boy, and I'll make us some coffee."

"Yes, sir."

"Uh!" Adler warned with an upraised finger.

"Right. Sorry."

Billy carried in enough deadwood, mesquite mostly, to make two fires. Adler already had a dented and fire-blackened old enamelware coffeepot filled with water fresh from the flow pipe. He added some ready-ground coffee and set the pot onto a fire ring left in place by past travelers.

Adler unwrapped a stack of cheese sandwiches he'd bought back at the railroad depot and handed one to Billy.

"Thanks." The sandwich was dry—it needed a thick

coating of butter like his mother used to make them—but a swallow of water cured that well enough.

"Did you think to bring a cup?"

"Yes, thanks."

Adler grunted again. He hunkered beside the fire and fiddled with the position of the coffepot, turning it so the handle faced the opposite of what it had been to start with. Not that Billy thought it needed changing, but then each man is entitled to his own way of doing things.

"You want some advice, boy?"

"Yes, sir. I'd be pleased to hear anything you want to tell me."

"That hogleg you're wearing."

"Yes, sir?"

"You got it riding high up on your waist. At least that way, you got it half right. Kids nowadays, they believe the crap they read in those yellow novels. Think they ought to wear a gun down low. Two things happen if you carry your gun down on your thigh. One is that when you get on a horse, 'specially if your horse gets to feeling frisky, your gun is gonna fall out. Maybe go off when it hits the ground too. Pretty soon these young'uns figure that out, so they use a thong to tie their guns into the holster. Know what that does for them? Makes it so they can't grab the thing and use it if trouble comes along. Might as well carry the thing down to the bank and ask them to lock it into the safe.

"Up there on the belt is where it needs to be. You can grab it there, and it isn't likely to drop out. But over there where you got it, there on your right side, you can grab it just fine with your right hand, but what happens if somebody has hold of that arm? Or some son of a bitch pinks you on that side? Same thing as before. Take your gun to the bank for safekeeping because you aren't gonna get it out without some delay.

"No, what you want to do is shift that holster around to the left of your belt buckle. It's every bit as easy to grab your gun out with your right hand as it is right now, and if need be you can always reach it instead with your left. It's much better over there."

Adler snorted and poured a little of the steaming but very pale coffee into his cup. He looked at it and tossed it onto the ground. "Not ready yet. Dammit. What was I saying? Oh, yes. Whatever you do, don't think you should carry in shoulder rigs like mine. They aren't that easy to handle. The movement to get at them isn't as natural as carrying at your belt. I do it from habit. Started so I could carry under my coat and some not notice that I was heeled. You don't need that. But do what I'm telling you here. Move that holster. And remember, if we get ourselves into a fight, there's some things you want to keep in mind. Best to sort them out right now so if such a time comes, you'll be prepared and know what you have to do.

"The first thing, boy, is that half the men I've killed were probably faster than I am and damn near all of them would've been better shots than me. What I had over them was an edge. Two, really. The first is that I always been prepared to kill a man.

"That's something I want you to think about. Lay awake at night and study on it, son. It could save your life someday. An awful lot of men will go into a gunfight and not really want to hurt the other man. That makes them slow to pull the trigger no matter how quick they may be getting their gun out of leather. I've had men stand there with their guns drawn ahead of me and look in my eyes and know I was going to kill them, and they still couldn't bring themselves to shoot." Adler shook his head. "Damnedest thing I ever did see, but I've seen it a lot more than once. So what you got to do, boy, is make peace with yourself over the fact that you can pull that trigger and send a bullet into a human person's gut. You got to be willing to make him bleed. You got to be willing to make him die. And you got to want the dying to be done by him and not by you. And don't think I'm not serious, for I am. Lie awake and think about this before you go to sleep nights. Prepare yourself in your mind against the time it could happen for real. Otherwise, you got no business wearing a gun. Guns are for shooting, not for scaring."

Adler chuckled and said, "Which brings me to the other point I want to make about fighting with guns. You want that other sonuvabitch to be just as scared as you know how to make him. Know how I do that, boy? I make noise."

"Sir?"

The gunfighter laughed. "I make noise. Shooting noise. Fast noise. I don't worry a thing about hitting anything with my first couple shots. I just want to grab iron and make fast noises. Scares hell out of the other fellow and nine times outa ten . . . no, make that ninety-nine times outa a hundred . . . he'll be so startled he'll just stand there trembling. Sometimes they even forget they got a gun of their own. They stand scared, and I have time then to work my next shots into their chest or their belly. I blow the first couple rounds off . . . doesn't matter where I put them . . . then concentrate on trying to hit the fella later. Sounds crazy, doesn't it? But it's so."

"You don't take close aim?" Billy asked.

"Naw. No need. Most gunfights, boy, take place as close as you are to me. Closer sometimes. But do you know what fear can do to a man?"

Adler paused, encouraging a response.

"No, sir, I don't."

"Boy, I have seen two grown men, both of them armed, stand close enough to reach out and touch each other on the chest. I've seen them draw their guns and empty them at each other. *And neither one gets hit!* Crazy damn thing, I tell you, but I've seen that with my own two eyes two, three different times." Adler shook his head. "Belly-to-belly. Five shots, each of them. And nobody hit." He laughed. "I'll tell you something else, boy. The times I've seen that happen, I've never yet seen anybody reload and try a second time. They've always turned and got the hell away just as fast as they could go, and generally with their britches wet too."

Billy wasn't sure if he should believe Mr. Adler about that or not. But he certainly sounded serious about it.

Billy loosened his belt and dragged his holster around so it hung to the left of his belt buckle. Mr. Adler was right about that. He could reach the .44 with either hand if need be.

"Get your cup. I think this coffee is ready now."

"Yes, sir. Thanks."

TWENTY-FIVE

AS far as Billy could determine, there wasn't a single structure in the entire town of Marly that would make a self-respecting chicken coop. The place wasn't so much a town as a collection of rock piles and dried mud, some of which had been arranged in the shape of buildings. Billy guessed there were several hundred people who found reason to live there, although he couldn't for the life of him figure out why anyone would want to.

"Handsome town, isn't it?" Adler said.

Billy peered at him, but could not decide if the man was serious or was pulling his leg.

Adler laughed. "Don't look so glum. There's work for us here, or so I was told. The word I hear is that there's Chinamen crossing over in broad daylight, right on that bridge over there." He nodded in the direction of a suspension footbridge that dangled from cables stretched across the Rio Grande.

"Soon as it gets around that we're here to put a stop to the traffic, the Chinamen will try and sneak in some other way. Count on it. So once we put a stop to the open crossing, we'll be setting up ambushes at the fords up and down the river from here. For the next little while, though, you and me will be working out of Marly."

Adler led the way onto the dusty main street that started at the United States end of the footbridge and ran an uneven northeasterly course among the stone and adobe buildings, until eventually it petered out in the mesquite and prickly-pear tangles in the surrounding countryside.

Marly had no hotel as such, but a saloon close to the river offered rooms to let in a courtyard behind the drinking establishment. Billy suspected the rooms were there for purposes other than meeting the needs of passing travelers, but there seemed to be no other options available in the town. Adler presented a pair of expense vouchers for their lodging, and had Billy sign one of them.

"There's a 'dobe corral over that way," the saloonkeeper said, inclining his head in the appropriate direction. "You can turn your horses in there free of charge. Feed 'em yourselves or if you'd ruther, I can have my boy carry hay to them. Ten cents per head per night. I can add that to these here pay papers if you like."

"We accept, thank you."

"Got no keys to the rooms, but if there's anything you don't want to leave untended, you can set it here behind the bar. Nobody'll bother it if it's here. Can't make any guarantees otherwise."

Adler nodded.

"Eat here too if you want. I'll add it on your bill. I can put a beer on too now an' then. After all, it comes with the lunch layout, an' you can call that a meal if you like. Whiskey you got to pay for cash on the counter. I've had troubles with the damned guv'ment about paying bar tabs before. I'm not going through that again. Same thing with women. Come dark there will be some plump Meskin gals in here. Don't ask me t' add them to your bill, for I won't do it." He shook his head. "Had a brand inspector down from McMullen County looking for stolen livestock. Got real huffy that I wouldn't put his whores on the guv'ment pay paper an' swore he'd never give me business again. Stuck to it too, he did. Course he got pretty uncomfortable sleeping out in the brush 'cause he made his declaration before he figured out I'm the only around here with rooms to let." The man gave them a wink and a grin.

"We'll keep your rules in mind," Adler promised.

"There's six rooms out there. Take any ones you want, but I'd recommend the ones in back if you expect any peace an' quiet. Won't be much of it there neither, but they're the best I have."

"We'll take those, thanks." Adler turned to Billy and said, "Come along then. We'll put our gear in the rooms, then you can take the horses over to the corral. Drop the saddles behind the bar there."

"Yes, sir." Billy wondered if his entire function would turn out to be tending to Mr. Adler's personal needs.

Not that he was complaining. Mr. Adler was the one with the worldly experience, and there was a lot Billy still had to learn.

And at seventy-five dollars a month and with the prospect of being able to support Edie as a wife should be . . . he could do pretty much anything as long as that bright dream lay on the horizon.

Soon as they got settled, he figured, he would sit down and write her a long letter, then find out where he could go to mail it. He hoped they would be here in Marly long enough to receive a reply from her. As it was, he was reading and rereading over and over the one letter he'd so far gotten from her.

Dang, but he was one mighty lucky fellow. A good job. And Edie waiting for him? Couldn't get any better than that, could it?

TWENTY-SIX

FUNNY, but until he reached El Paso just a few weeks ago, he never in his life had seen electric lights, horseless carriages, or electrified streetcars.

Now he kinda missed them.

Actually, he couldn't be sure the people of Marly had yet *heard* about any of those things. Marly seemed to him a throwback to the Wild West days he'd always read about. It was kind of fitting, he thought, that a man like Tuck Adler would be here.

Even so, he felt like a fraud to be here with a badge pinned to his shirt and a revolver at his waist. Like a fraud or an actor on a stage where it was all playacting and nothing was real. Mr. Adler was the real thing. But he himself was just plain Billy Delisle.

He pondered that over a dinner of goat stew and tortillas, then remained at the table with his pen and paper while Adler moved to the other side of the room to a low-stakes poker game and a bottle of cheap spirits.

Billy finished his letter to Edie, and sat a few moments longer visualizing her lovely face . . . and remembering the feel of her so sweet and trusting in his arms . . . until Adler broke his reverie.

"The women are here, kid. Pick one. And don't worry about the money. I'll take care of that for you until you get some pay in your pocket."

Billy felt the heat leap into his cheeks. A prickly sensation flooded the back of his neck, and his shoulders became almost too heavy to carry. Very carefully, he kept his eyes away from the back of the room, where he now could hear the chirp and flutter of female voices. "I . . . I . . . couldn't do that, sir."

"Sure you could, you . . . say now, son, you aren't a virgin, are you?"

Billy was sure Adler shouted that last part loud enough for everyone in the place to overhear. He felt like crawling underneath the table.

"Now I'm pretty sure you aren't one of those poof-boys, kid, 'cause you haven't been trying to sneak into my blankets nor peek at me naked. You really are a virgin, aren't you? Shee-it! Come on back here, son. Let's get your ashes hauled. It'll improve your whole outlook, boy." He laughed. "Trust me."

Adler took hold of Billy's shoulder, but Billy resisted the man's nudge. "I . . . I have a girl. Back home. We're engaged to be married, sort of."

"Hell, everybody's married, kid. But didn't you know? Married only counts within fifteen miles of home. Anything past that and you're single again." He laughed again, louder this time, and tried once more to drag Billy toward the back of the saloon.

Billy heard footsteps, and became aware of the scent of sweat and cloyingly sweet perfume.

"Rosa, take this boy and show him how to do it, will you, honey?" Adler said. Without lowering his voice, he added, "My partner's never been with a woman. Can you imagine that?"

Billy felt another hand touch him. On the back of the neck this time. He cringed. He wanted not even to look, but his eyes betrayed him. Rosa was young and plump and pretty. She had shiny black hair and soft, billowy breasts that she pressed against Billy's right ear and cheek when she leaned over him. He could smell . . . he could feel. . . .

He panicked. Bolted from his chair and with the letter to Edie clutched tight in his hand, he ran outside, leaving the sounds of laughter—all of it directed toward him, he was positive—in the saloon behind him.

He was shaking so badly that for the first several yards he could scarcely walk.

He went down to the riverbank and found a jumble of rocks to sit on while he struggled to get himself in order.

The bad thing, the really horrid thing, was that he'd been tempted. He sat there looking out over the Rio Grande and tried to keep his thoughts firmly fixed on prayer and Edith Forester.

After a while, he was able to claim victory in that effort. His trembling ceased and his breathing eased. He stood and went to see if he could find a place to mail his letter.

TWENTY-SEVEN

THE sky to the east was turning pink with the new dawn when Tuck Adler came rapping on Billy's door.

"Wake up there, kid. Rise and shine. We have work to do."

Billy rubbed the sleep from his eyes and pulled his britches on. He stepped into his boots, buttoned his shirt, and rinsed his mouth with some of the water from a pitcher on the bedside stand. He buckled his revolver into place and picked up his hat. "Where're we off to?" he asked.

Adler grinned. "Breakfast."

"But I thought. . . ."

"And so we will, boy. Everything in its own time. But first we'll have something to eat, quick before I starve. Then I'm going to have a shave"—he squinted and peered closely at Billy for a moment—"though it looks like you won't be needing one yet. Then we shall see what we shall see, right?"

Billy had always been given to understand that a man paid a heavy price on the dreaded "morning after" when he'd enjoyed a night of debauchery. That might very well be, as some of Billy's friends back home attested, but Mr. Adler gave every impression of feeling chipper and happy and raring to go. If he was hung over and addlepated, he was doing a manful job of hiding his discomfort.

Adler led the way into the saloon, where a few men stood at the bar drinking beer. Billy could not tell if they were there still, or were there already.

He had a yen for ham and eggs and fried potatoes for breakfast, but it turned out there was no menu to choose from. One had breakfast or one didn't. So they broke their fast with beans, tortillas, and chunks of barely cooked bacon, all washed down with strong, steaming-hot coffee. The good thing was that Billy liked all of those offerings and so had no complaint.

"You might've thought I was just raising a little Ned and having myself a good time last night," Adler said around a mouthful of bacon. He winked. "And if the truth be known, boy, I was damn sure doing that. But I also got us a start on our work here."

"How'd you do a thing like that, sir?"

"I put the word around that we're Federal officers here to see to the border. Now I don't figure this is gonna put us any Chinamen in the bag, mind. But I figure it will stop the traffic across that bridge down the road. They won't be so damned open about flaunting the law from here on. That will limit them to the fords. This time of year, the water's low enough there's several places where a man on foot can come across without having to swim. It will be up to us to find those places and settle on some spots we can watch them from. You with me about this?"

"Yes, sir, I think so." Adler was either too preoccupied to notice Billy's return to "sir" as a form of address, or had decided to accept what he was unable to change, for he was not objecting to it much anymore.

"Once we know where we need to keep watch, we'll split up. One of us go upstream, the other down. We'll find spots to hide and wait . . . in the shade, I damn sure hope . . . and let the damned Chinamen come to us, don't you see."

"When they do, do we arrest them?"

"And do what with them? The government doesn't want the slant-eyed bastards. It just wants to keep them out. No, when we find them, we'll just chase them back into Mexico. Let the Meskins do whatever they like with them over there. It won't be any of our worry long as they stay that side of the river. Of course if anybody, one o' their guides for instance, since we'll be taking cash money away from them by stopping this illegal traffic, if somebody wants to get growly with you, then you can arrest him and bring him back here to Marly. Or shoot him if that looks the better idea."

"Just . . . shoot him down?"

"Well, you'd need justification, of course. Like if he moved his hand. And mind, once he's dead he can't testify *why* he moved. Keep that in mind. If you're gonna shoot him, make sure you kill him. Makes things easier on everybody if you go ahead an' do that." Adler shoveled another heaping spoonful of red beans into his mouth and began chewing.

"Y-yes, sir," Billy mumbled with no conviction whatsoever. He was not convinced he could shoot another human being under any circumstances. Certainly he would never be able to do it as callously as Adler was suggesting.

Adler ate quickly, finishing his meal when Billy was only half done with his. The older man stood, stretched, and let out a loud belch. "That was good. Tell you what, kid. I'm going down to the barbershop. Do you remember it?"

"Yes, sir, I think so."

"Right straight up the street on the other side. You'll see it. I'm gonna go ahead and get my shave. Take your time here and come join me once you're done, hear?"

"All right."

Adler tugged at the lapels of his coat and set the battered and famous old derby hat at a rakish angle before he marched out into the now-bright morning sunlight.

Billy stayed where he was, toying pensively at his beans. He was feeling too preoccupied at the moment to be thinking about food, good though it was.

TWENTY-EIGHT

THE oppressive weight of the sun hadn't yet descended on them. The morning air was comfortable, if not exactly cool. All in all, Billy had no complaints, at least not with the weather. He ambled up the street toward the striped pole in the distance that signaled the presence of a barber-shop.

People were beginning to move around, perhaps doing their shopping early so as to avoid the heat that would come in another hour or so. Merchants were already open for business. Doors were open and fly-beads hung. Billy paused once to admire a pair of handsomely stitched boots in the shoemaker's window, and again to peep in at a haberdasher's.

He had never owned a shirt sewn by anyone other than his mother. Some of them looked pretty nice, but he did not have courage enough to go inside and inquire about prices.

When he began receiving pay, he wanted first to pay Mr. Adler what he owed him, then start putting money by for the needs of the future. It was going to cost quite a bit, he suspected, to find a place for him and Edie to live once they were married. They would have to meet the rent and buy some furniture and kitchen things and like that, he supposed. He wondered just how much he ought to have before he asked Edie to set a date and make her plans for the wedding.

A lady's hat in another window caught his eye and he stopped to look at it, imagining it on Edie's pretty head. Lordy, but he was lucky to have a girl like her waiting for him.

Billy was smiling when he approached the barbershop. The place must be awfully full at this hour, he thought, for there were several men standing outside, one leaning against the wall on either side of the door.

The two men nodded a hello to him as he approached, then for some reason, the nearer of them scowled and said something to the other.

Billy passed between them into the barbershop. There were two chairs and two barbers, both busy at the moment. But while there were men waiting to be served, there were three empty chairs in the room where those gents outside could have sat.

Mr. Adler was in the right-hand chair, a striped sheet arranged over him to protect his clothes and his face half covered with lather. The barber, a squat man with dark features and white hair, carefully scraped at Adler's whiskers with a straight razor that was so worn away from years of sharpening that it might well have come over on the boat with Columbus.

Billy looked at the empty chairs, frowned, and glanced back toward the two who were loitering at the doorway.

They were looking inside, and his skeptical look spooked them.

Both men drew their guns.

Billy couldn't believe it. He stood rooted in place, gaping and wondering. A robbery? Why would anyone bother to rob a barbershop? And what were—

A sequence of loud explosions battered his eardrums. The sheet over Mr. Adler puffed outward in a weird sort of dance, and it caught fire in a couple different places.

Mr. Adler came off the barber chair charging straight at the two men in the doorway, a pistol in each hand and cold fury in his eyes.

The men in the doorway were as immobile with shock and surprise as Billy was. They had their revolvers already in hand, but neither one seemed to think about shooting back. They stood there motionless long enough for Adler to stop his wild firing and take deliberate aim. He pumped a bullet into the nearer man's chest, then shot the other low in the belly.

Billy could see puffs of dust fly up where the bullets hit.

He expected a lot of blood, but there was none. Not right away.

The man who'd been shot in the chest fell to the floor right away, but the other one staggered backward, tripped when he came to the edge of the board sidewalk, and fell heavily into the street.

He'd expected blood? Oh, there was aplenty of blood flowing now. The man who fell inside the barbershop was bleeding as bad as a shoat with its throat slashed. The sticky, stinking stuff ran onto the barber's floor and formed a huge puddle inside the doorway. Customers who had been waiting for their morning shaves began to shift away from the spreading scarlet pool, and one of them added to the mess by puking into it.

Within seconds, the shop emptied save for Billy and Mr. Adler and one of the two barbers. The would-be customers fled. Out the back way.

Billy's head ached and his ears rang and his nose was filled with the sharply sour stench of black powder fired in an enclosed space.

Mr. Adler calmly reloaded his short-barreled Colts, shucking the empty brass shells onto the barbershop floor. He had to retrieve his coat from the rack beside the door in order to get fresh cartridges. He seemed not to mind wading through the congealing blood in order to get there.

Billy wanted to throw up himself, but he held it in. He was supposed to be an officer of the law too. Wasn't he?

Right at this moment, he was not so sure that he wanted to be.

Two men. Dead. Or anyway dying. The one inside was surely dead. The one lying in the street seemed to be moving a little.

Adler finished reloading, bent down to check on the dead one, then stepped over his body to go outside.

Billy wanted to go with him. But he did not at all want to walk through all that blood to get there. He stood where he was, unwilling to abandon his partner by heading for the back door, but unable to bring himself to step into the blood.

Adler stood on the sidewalk looking down at the dying man.

"Don't move, Carl," Adler said in a strong voice loud

enough to carry from one end of the block to the other. "Don't try it. *No!*"

He shouted the warning. Then took slow, careful aim and fired into the dying man's face.

Billy was not close enough to see very well. And for that he was entirely grateful.

The .45 slug landed somewhere in the vicinity of the bridge of Carl's nose and more or less caved the front of his face in.

Billy could not see, did not want to see, did not want even to imagine the horrors that took place when the bullet came out the other side.

"You saw him move, didn't you?" Adler said as he turned back to Billy. "You saw him try for me, right?"

Adler once again flicked open the loading gate on his revolver and dumped an empty cartridge onto the floor, carefully reloading before he shoved that pistol back into its slick-leather underarm rig.

Billy peeped outside. Then wheeled and made a dive for the waste bucket where the barbers put hair clippings.

His breakfast tasted terrible coming back up.

TWENTY-NINE

"NEVER saw anything like that before, kid? Don't worry. You'll get used to it."

"If it's all the same with you, sir, I'd rather not get used to something like that. I thought we were just going to find Chinese fellas and chase them back away from the border. I didn't think there would be anything like . . . like that."

They were back in the saloon, Adler having a drink to fortify himself for the day, while Billy tried to wash the foul taste out of his mouth with a beer and some pickled eggs and cheese. After throwing up, he felt hollowed out and empty.

"Mr. Adler, shouldn't we . . . I don't know . . . call in the local police or report to the sheriff or . . . something?"

Adler laughed. "Boy, you and me are all the law there is for a good fifty, sixty miles around. I'll write down a report for the major when we get back to El Paso. In the meantime, we'll just get about doing our job."

"Why did those men grab iron and come for you, Mr. Adler? You knew at least that one. Was this something from the past catching up with you here or what?"

"I'd tell you if I could, boy, but the truth is that with those two dead, we'll likely never really know why they did a boneheaded thing like that." He snorted. "If I do say so, taking after me face-on was pretty damn boneheaded too. I'd've expected their kind to wait and get me from ambush, or at least one in front and the other one behind. My guess is that they were waiting outside to do just that. Then they saw your badge and figured you were gonna warn me and there'd be two of us to stand up to the two of them. Their kind don't like even odds. They'd want an edge. Prob'ly figured I wouldn't be ready for them with my face half shaved."

Adler fingered his chin. "Come to think of it, I still need this other side shaved." He laughed. "But I don't think I'll ask that barber man to hold a razor up tight to my throat again until he's had some time to settle down.

"Anyway, you were asking about those two. The one of them was Carl Witkin. He wasn't such a bad old boy. From up around Gilmer, I think he was. Next time we get to a telegraph, remind me to send a wire to the sheriff there so Carl's kin can be told what happened to him.

"The other one was named Amos. I don't know his last name or much about him, but I've seen him one place and another. You could say him and me tended to run in the same circles although on opposite sides of things.

"Carl and Amos were mostly thieves, kid. Dealt a lot in stolen livestock. Maybe they thought we were here to put a stop to whatever it was they were doing down here, and they wanted to get me before I could catch them at something.

"The pity of it is that it isn't our job to care about brand inspections or rustled stock or anything like that. All we care about is the border and that no Chinamen cross it.

"You see that bridge out there. There's no guards looking to see what passes over it. Folks can come and go however they please between Mexico and the U.S. And they can carry whatever goods they like when they cross. That isn't what you and me were hired to watch out for.

"Makes it all the more of a waste that Carl and Amos came after us, doesn't it?"

"Yes, sir, I expect that it does. Could I ask you something else then?"

"Of course. Anything. There's no secrets between partners, boy, so you feel free to ask whatever you please."

"That Carl fellow. He was still alive. Did you have to put him down like you did?"

"Yes, I did, son. For a couple reasons. First off, I hope you saw his gun hand move. He was still holding that hogleg of his, and I couldn't take a chance that he wouldn't get a shot off.

"Second, Carl was gutshot. He could have lingered a week or longer, in worse agony than mortal man should ought to bear. He was gonna die, no two ways about it, and he would've been in terrible pain every minute until he kicked off. So you could say that I did him a powerful favor by seeing to it that he didn't suffer no more'n he had to.

"Thirdly, I was doing exactly what I told you had to be done. When you've had to shoot a man, make sure of him.

Take no chances with him. He could get to you before he dies. Sure thing he'll want to. And sometimes it's lies he'll use for his weapon. If a man can't put you down with his pistol, he'll sometimes try and take you out with his tongue. Tell wild, awful stories. Made-up stuff. Likely no one will believe him, but it don't take all that much to get rumors started and ruin a man's reputation. No, boy, the fact is that if you're gonna kill a man, you're just plain better off to get it over and done with."

Billy pondered that advice. He could not claim he agreed with it. But at least Mr. Adler had reasons for what he'd done.

And maybe Carl really had moved, really had wanted to make a dying attempt to shoot Mr. Adler out there.

Maybe.

"Want another beer, kid?"

"No, I . . . yes. Yes, dammit, I do."

"Stay there. I'll bring it when I get a refill for myself."

THIRTY

Dear Miss Forester:

I write to you from the banks of the Rio Grande River where my partner and I seek out the crossing points. From these points we shall spy out the would-be Chinese emigrants. Immigrants? I can never keep those two straight in my mind. Forgive my ignorance, please. I plead abstraction on the grounds that my thoughts today, indeed every hour of every day, remain fixed upon you.

It is my hope that you have not lost faith with me nor interest. I have gone many days without receiving any letter from you. Perhaps you no longer care to write. I pray this is not the reason and that your mail if any has but been delayed inroot.

You will see upon the outside of this envelope the address where I may be found for the coming weeks. If *you continue to have feelings for me, Miss Forester, I beg the indulgence of your time and effort so as to send an epistle to me.*

Would it be overly bold of me to offer you a suvenir of my presence here on the border? I hope it would not. On the Mexcan side of same I only yesterday saw a quite fetching cameo brooch set upon a black velvet ribbon. The brooch is now wrapped with tender care and deposited within my bedroll where it will be close to my heart until next I have the distinct pleasure of casting my eyes upon the One whose health and happiness I most desire.

I see my foolscap is soon used up, my dear Miss Forester, and so I shall close my letter to you. But never will I cease from thinking of you and imagining your grace and beauty.

Please accept my warmest regards for yrself and for all your family.

With fond regards,
William Delisle

THIRTY-ONE

"LOOK, kid, we have a tough job ahead of us. There's only the two of us, and there's a couple hundred miles of border between us and the next team of agents, right?"

Billy nodded. He supposed that was right, although each team was pretty much free to go where they wanted in their efforts to keep the Chinese out of the country.

"I think our best bet is to split up. I been watching you, and I'm satisfied you can be trusted to do your duty with or without supervision."

Billy felt a small glow of satisfaction at the compliment, but kept his mouth shut and tried not to show his feelings on the grounds that that would not be the mature and professional thing to do.

"I want you to keep watch over the ford south of town." Over the past few days of scouting up and down the Rio Grande from Marly, they'd found one good ford located

about seven miles south of the town and two other crossing points to the north, one within two miles, but the other
at least twelve miles upstream.

"That is gonna be your assignment for the next little
while. You should ride down there in the morning an' come
back here to sleep. You can lay up in that patch of brush we
found and look down on the ford. You'll be able to see a
good ways off if any Chinamen are coming. If they do,
mind you have to wait until they come across the river to
the U.S. side before you show yourself. Far as we
know . . . or anyway, as far as we care . . . they got every
right to be in Mexico. What they do over there is none of
our business, right?"

"Yes, sir."

"So just stay hid until they get on the U.S. side of the
river. Then draw your gun and brace them. There will be
Meskin or maybe American guides with them. Remember,
it's the guides that could give you trouble. If there's any
doubt in your mind at all, don't think about it. Just shoot.
Better yet . . . now I think about it, I'm gonna stop at the
hardware this afternoon an' buy you a rifle. A good repeater in . . . what cartridges do you use in that Smith?"

Billy told him.

"Fine. I'll find you a saddle carbine in .44-40. It uses
the same cartridge as your pistol, but it has longer range
and better accuracy. Not so quick to get into action, of
course. You don't have to worry about that since you'll be
the one with the advantage. You wait until they're on our
side of the river, then cover the guides. Turn the Chinamen
back and shoot the guides." Adler presumably saw Billy's
reaction to that instruction because he added, "Or you can
arrest them and bring them back here. Whichever seems

the better idea to you at the time. But I'm telling you plain as plain can be, boy. Don't take chances. There will only be one of you and could be two or three of them. If their horses' ears twitch, shoot the guides. It will keep them from shooting you, don't you see."

"Yes, sir." But he was not sure if he meant it. "If I'll be alone at that south ford, will you be at one of the ones to the north then?"

"That's right. I'll divide my time between them. It isn't a perfect plan. I suppose a bunch of Chinese could slip by since between us we can only cover the two places at any one time, but I'll be able to keep an eye out for tracks, so if anything happens while I'm not there I'll have a pretty good idea of it. If I think there's a bunch of them has sneaked past, the two of us can take after them the next day. I'm told these Chinamen are brought over on foot, so they won't be moving fast. Anyway, we'll do our best." Adler smiled. "Won't we?"

"Yes, sir, we surely will."

"That's right, we will."

Later, when Adler stopped in at Billy's room to deliver a used but not abused Marlin repeater and several boxes of ammunition, the senior agent told him, "You'd best count on having supper by yourself tonight. I'm gonna go across the river to the Mex side. Nose around and see what I can see about any Chinamen over there waiting to slip across. I'll prob'ly find some fat little senorita and spend the night there, then ride up along the Meskin side to see what the conditions are like over there. I'll cross the lower ford to get back over here and spend the day setting up my ambushes. I'll plan on seeing you back here tomorrow night and get your report on what you saw to the south. All right?"

"Yes, sir. Thanks for letting me know."

"We're partners, boy. There's no secrets between partners. Never." Adler's smile was reassuring.

"Yes, sir. You can count on me."

"I've never had the least doubt about that." He turned to leave, then paused at the door and said, "You might want to carry a lunch with you tomorrow and one of those boxes of cartridges. Take a little time and get used to that carbine before you need to rely on it."

"Won't noise spook the Chinese and their guides?"

Adler shrugged. "Our job is to turn them back. If we can do it by making a little noise, I don't see that as a problem."

Billy grinned. He didn't say anything to Mr. Adler about it. But if he saw any Chinese and guides fixing to cross the river, well, that might be a just-fine time for him to undertake a little target practice.

"Good night, sir."

"G'night, boy. See you back here tomorrow night."

THIRTY-TWO

MR. Adler had said the Chinese came across the border on foot. Billy remembered that quite distinctly. On foot. The people he saw on the Mexican side of the river were mounted, and there were only two . . . no, there was a third coming out of the brush now.

The three riders came down to the riverbank and sat there for a while peering across to the Texas side. Then one bumped his horse down into the water.

The animal obviously was not happy about being asked to get itself wet. Over and over it tried to turn back, but each time the rider patiently spun it around until it once more was pointed toward Texas and gigged it in the ribs. Eventually, the horse gave in and splashed into the belly-deep river.

The animal emerged on the American side a minute or so later, stopped to brace its legs wide apart and shake itself like a dog. The rider bent down, said something to his horse, and patted the side of its neck. The horse, a stocky little brown with fuzzy ears and a tail cropped unusually short, scrambled up the slope of the bank to the more or less level ground about the ford.

At that point, it wasn't thirty yards from where Billy had made himself a comfortable spy post in the shade of some drooping mesquite. He had staked his horse behind a pile of rock a couple furlongs to the north so it was out of sight.

The fellow on horseback took his time looking around, standing in his stirrups and craning his neck so he could see whatever there was to see. Then he turned back and rode to the top of the riverbank. He removed his hat and waved it in a wide circle above his head.

A couple minutes after that, Billy could see some dust rise out of the brush on the Mexican side, and then a string of skinny cattle came stepping one by one into view, accompanied by the two riders Billy had already seen over there, plus one more fellow who must have stayed back with the cattle while the first three were looking things over.

Billy had no doubt whatsoever about what he was seeing now. Those four men were cow thieves. They'd stolen these beeves somewhere on the Mexican side, and now they intended to bring them across into Texas, either to sell them for a quick profit or brand them and keep them. Billy couldn't see from this far away if the beeves were steers or cows, but it didn't really matter what the intention was. The cattle were stolen and that meant the men were thieves.

And Billy Delisle was an officer of the law. Sort of.

The steel badge pinned to his shirt felt heavy, and his mouth was dry.

He was only out here to stop Chinese from illegally entering the United States. That was what he was being paid for.

But the major had said they were bona fide law officers.

And right out there were a bunch of bona fide thieves trying to bring stolen livestock into the United States. Eighteen, twenty . . . twenty-three head, Billy counted.

He didn't know why he was counting the cattle as they plodded single file down the bank and into the river.

It was just something to occupy his mind, he supposed. Something other than the worry about what he was supposed to do about the four men who were with those beeves.

His mouth was dry and his hands were sweaty and he was finding it kind of hard to make himself swallow. He could feel his heart thumping and banging inside his chest hard enough to make the badge jump.

He'd sworn an oath, hadn't he?

And he was an officer of the law, wasn't he?

He looked out from his hiding place at the cow thieves. The one who had come ahead to this side of the river was a white man. He dressed like a regular cowboy with a faded blue bandanna and collarless shirt and a wide-brimmed hat. He'd patted his horse's neck. Was that the sort of thing a thief would do? Thieves were supposed to be surly and mean and ugly, weren't they? This cowboy didn't look any older than Billy.

The first of the cattle reached Texas and began to walk up onto dry ground, the first of the men with them. Billy could see that that one was a black man. He too was dressed like a regular person. He looked to be older than the fellow who' d come over to scout the way. He had a short beard.

All of them, Billy saw, carried pistols on their belts, including the ones still in the water.

Oh, God. What was he supposed to do now?

Sit where he was? Let them come across with their stolen cattle?

And what if they were just a bunch of cowboys on a perfectly legitimate mission? Maybe these cattle had somehow strayed over onto the Mexican side, and these riders were just bringing them back where they belonged. Maybe they'd gone over and bought the cattle. Maybe they had a properly executed bill of sale for these animals. Maybe there was no reason Billy should bother them now. No reason he should even show himself. He was here looking for Chinese people, not scrawny little Mexican cattle that hadn't ever been upgraded from the old-time longhorn blood.

He might not have any right at all to bother these fellows.

The third man came out of the water. He was a white man, older than the others, with gray in his beard.

The fourth, Billy could see now, was dark-skinned, although at this distance he couldn't tell if the man was perhaps a Mexican or another black man.

There were the four of them. And twenty-three cattle. And just one Billy Delisle here at the crossing from Mexico into the United States.

The thing was . . . Billy had that badge on his shirt. And he'd sworn an oath as an officer of the law.

He felt dizzy and sick to his stomach, and he wished he

was anywhere in the world other than right here and right now.

He stood up.

He took a step. And then another. Out of his shaded concealment into the bright glare of the afternoon sun.

THIRTY-THREE

MR. Adler was about to fall off his damn chair. Billy kind of wished that he would. Fall off and bust his tailbone. At least that would hush him up.

"I can't . . . I can't . . . can't believe . . . oh, dear. Oh, my. I can't believe . . . oh, it hurts. My belly hurts."

The man was laughing so hard, it was a wonder he didn't wet himself. Probably it would be better if he did. Maybe that would make him quit laughing.

"I can't believe . . . oh . . . my side." He guffawed and hoorahed and yelped loud enough to wake the dead. He wriggled. He squirmed. He clutched hold of his belly and doubled over, moaning and carrying on.

"You told them . . . you really told them . . . stand and deliver?"

"It's the only thing I could think of right at the moment," Billy sheepishly admitted.

"That's something . . . oh, this hurts . . . that's something the outlaws say, Billy." As best Billy could remember, that was the first time Mr. Adler ever bothered to speak to him by his actual name. Under the circumstances, it was an honor he would have gladly delayed yet a while longer.

"I know that wasn't the right thing to call out," Billy said. "I just didn't know what to holler. So I opened my mouth and that's what came out."

"Oh, dear. I love it." Adler straightened in his chair and managed to wipe the tears out of his eyes and off his cheeks. "Oh, my. Stand and deliver," he cackled. "Stand and deliver."

It might very well have been funny, Billy thought. If it'd been happening to somebody else.

"Stand and deliver," Adler gasped. He wiped his eyes again and took a healthy pull at the glass of whiskey on the table between them. "Stand and deliver." He sighed and got a little better control of himself. "Tell me again what those cow thieves did then."

"Aw, shit, sir. I already told you."

"No, really. I have to make an official report about this, you know."

"Just . . . there oughtn't to be any need for that surely."

"Tell me again anyhow. I'll decide later what to put in the report to turn in to the major."

"Yes, sir," Billy said with considerable reluctance. "Like I told you, I stepped out to where they could see me and I hollered . . . well, you know what I hollered."

Adler grinned and bobbed his head and laughed some more. He waved his hand in a beckoning motion as a gesture for Billy to continue reporting what had happened out there beside the Rio Grande ford.

"I hollered what I did, and then I fired a shot into the air to make sure they could see that I had a gun on them. And it was like I'd kicked a wasp's nest.

"The one nearest to me shouted something, a warning for his pals, I guess, and bent down over the withers of that horse. He put the spurs to the critter and went larruping the hell outa there just as quick as his horse could pick them up and put them down. Didn't look to see where he was going or anything. Just threw the spurs to that horse and went straight ahead as hard as he could go.

"The black man riding behind him pulled a pistol and started shooting. Let loose a full cylinder of cartridges, I'd say, and I got no idea what he was shooting at. Into the air mostly, I think. For sure, he wasn't looking my way. He was just shooting, kind of in general, if you know what I mean.

"By that time, with all the commotion going on, the cattle were off on a tear. They headed south, raising dust and flinging busted branches and twigs and stuff in the air. They were running like they wouldn't slow down till they got to the Gulf of Mexico. And maybe not then, except they'd have to swim once they hit the water.

"The white man with the beard, he didn't waste any time messing with shooting or anything. He just wheeled his horse and headed back toward Mexico, leaping and splashing like a big-ass fish; he was half under water what with all the waves he was creating. I never knew a horse could run like that when it was belly-deep.

"And the last man, the other dark-skinned one, he shriveled up like he'd puckered himself near about inside his own butt. Making himself small, I suppose, while he turned around and took off toward the Mexican side of the river at a tiptoe. I think maybe he thought I wouldn't so easy notice him if he sneaked away.

"The first one, he was headed inland. The cows were stampeding downriver. The black man ran out of bullets and started racing after the first man. And those other two by then were back across into Mexico."

Billy took a deep breath. "Sorry, sir. I messed up, didn't I?"

"Aw, hell, kid. You did all right. You didn't shoot anybody and nobody shot you." Adler grinned. "And no Chinamen crossed over into the U.S. So you did your job." The grin turned into a broad, beaming smile. "More or less. What was it you hollered at them again?"

"Mr. Adler you know damn good and well what I said."

Adler began laughing again, although maybe not quite so loud. "Next time, Billy, next time tell them something on the order of 'Halt in the name of the law.' Or words to that effect. Pretty much anything." The grin shined off his face again. "Anything except 'Stand and deliver,' that is."

The man broke up laughing and grabbed at his no-doubt aching side.

Billy glanced down at the polished steel badge on his shirt. He was sure he could see Mr. Adler's laughing face reflected on the shield.

THIRTY-FOUR

COME morning, Billy was still feeling troubled. He hadn't handled himself well yesterday, and Mr. Adler was right to laugh at him. But . . . now what?

Over breakfast he worked up courage enough to pose a question. He probably would not have, except Mr. Adler had calmed down enough after all the hoorahing that maybe he could be serious again.

"I've been wondering, sir. What should I do about all those cattle now? Should I run them down today? I'm pretty sure I'd be able to find them."

Adler grunted and took a swallow of coffee before he answered. "Leave your post unmanned and go find those cows? What for? Whose cows are they? Who would you turn them over to? And where? Did you see their brand?"

Billy shook his head.

"You can't just go riding around gathering up cows that might not even be the ones you saw out there yesterday."

Billy was pretty sure he could in fact find and identify those particular cattle. Mr. Adler didn't seem to know all that much about cows and cowboying, but Billy was confident he could find the right bunch if he went looking for them. He knew a little bit about cows and tracking, after all, and he'd gotten a good look at the animals even if not at their brands. He would recognize them if he saw them again.

Still, Mr. Adler was right in that Billy could not possibly know who the cattle belonged to. It could be anyone. On either side of the border.

Under the circumstances, it was even possible, as he'd considered to his horror during the night hours, that those fellows he'd braced yesterday could have bought the cattle over in Mexico all legal and proper and just been taking them home to their own place.

Of course, if that were the fact, they would be perfectly capable of coming back and finding the missing cows themselves.

If he saw them again, he decided, he wouldn't say a word. Not one single word. He didn't want a repeat of that rodeo he'd started yesterday.

Adler chewed on his breakfast for a while, then pushed his empty plate away and rocked back in his chair. "You know, boy, you didn't do as bad out there as you might be thinking."

"Sir?"

"You did all right really. You accepted your responsibility as a peace officer, and you did something about it. At the risk of your own life."

"Me?" He shook his head. "It wasn't anything like that."

"Didn't you tell me that one rider was shooting at you?"

"He was just shooting. I don't know that he even saw where I was standing."

"Bull! He was shooting. You stood up to him. You didn't turn tail and run. That's good, boy. Real good. I'm proud of you. If I was gonna make a suggestion for how you can improve, it would be next time don't shoot into the air. Drop the nearest rider with a bullet in the brisket. That will get the attention of the rest of them. And do it from behind cover. You don't have to step out to where they can see you. Shoot the sonuvabitch off his horse, then have at the rest of them before they can get their wits about them."

"What if they're local ranchers coming home from buying cows in Mexico?"

"They won't be. Not in empty country like this," Adler asserted with no hint of doubt or error in his voice.

"I couldn't do that, sir. I just couldn't."

"That's up to you. You got the right to handle yourself however you think best. But don't be surprised if some cow thief puts a bullet in your belly while you're standing there asking him for his bill of sale."

"Yes, sir. I agree that I got to do this as best as I see fit."

Adler tilted his head to one side and squinted across the table for a moment. "You got sand in you, Billy. I'll say that for you."

"Thank you, sir. D'you want me to go back to that same spot today?"

Adler nodded. "Every day. You take the south; I'll

cover the north; between us there shouldn't ought to be any Chinamen come across this border. Now let's us collect the sack lunches that's supposed to be ready for us, and we'll get down to work."

"Yes, sir, I'm right behind you."

THIRTY-FIVE

On the Border, 26th inst.
   Dear Miss Forester:
   *I write to you today from ambush. Ha ha. If there is
one good thing to be said for my duty assignment, it is
that I have ample time while lurking beside the Rio
Grande River to lay my saddle across my lap and use
it as a desk so that I may write to you. That will
explain, I hope, why this missive is written with a lead
pencil rather than the customary pen and ink.*

   *My partner says we will guard these same crossing
points over the river for some time to come, so I
should be able to write to you often. I shall do so in
the great hope that you will be kind enough to
reciprocate. Every day, my dearest Miss Forester (may
I be so boldly forward as to so address you?), my
thoughts dwell upon you. Every evening when I return*

to our quarters, I do so with the eager hope that I shall receive a letter from you in the day's post. Every waking moment, it is the memory of your lovely face that lies before me. I see you in the clouds of the sky and in the ripples upon the surface of the moving water. I see you all about me, Miss Forester, yet I ache to be able once more to see you in person. To hear your voice. To touch your hand. To bask in your presence.

May I bore you with a story from my work? Yesterday I accosted a band of cow thieves who were attempting to bring stolen livestock into the United States. It was the first such "action" I have seen, and while gunshots were fired, no one came to harm, myself included. The thieves were able to effect their escape, but they did so without the stolen beeves. My partner claims he is well pleased with this performance.

It is my earnest hope, Miss Forester, that this letter will find you and yrs in abundant good health.

And it is my hope as well that your feelings and intentions are unchanged since last we spoke. If you have second thoughts, please be kind enough to tell me at the earliest possible date for my thoughts, my hopes, my dreams all center upon you, dearest Edith Jane.

Please know that I remain and always shall be, sincerely yours,

(Billy)

William Delisle, Mounted Agent

THIRTY-SIX

BILLY stood up and stomped his feet. His left foot had gone to sleep, and the pins-and-needles tingle itched something awful as his blood began circulating again. He balanced on his right foot alone, and tried to avoid putting any weight on the prickly left. That helped a little, but he very nearly fell down.

As soon as he felt like walking on that foot again, he figured, he would saddle up and head for Marly. He wanted to get back before dark for he wasn't yet sure of this country and would purely hate to get himself lost. Mr. Adler would have a fine laugh out of that if he did.

Not that a fellow could get so terribly lost considering there was only one river in the neighborhood, and he could get back to Marly simply by following that. Sticking close beside the riverbank was not necessarily all that good an idea, though. There were some gullies and washouts that would be a real nuisance to cross if it came dark before he got back, and making all the twists and turns of the river would add several miles onto the trip. Better to go on in, he thought.

It certainly wasn't like he was doing any good out here. Apart from trash floating by in the river, the only things he'd seen moving all afternoon were a few turkey vultures, a jackrabbit, and a couple coyotes. If he'd been back home, he probably would have tried to shoot those coyotes. They would kill lambs and calves and chickens and such and were considred vermin. Down here, though, well, he just didn't much feel like shooting some living something. The sheep and goats that were supposed to use this country— of which he had as yet seen exactly none anyway—were some other fellow's problem. Let *him* shoot the coyotes if he wanted them killed.

Billy yawned and stepped gingerly down on the left foot. He decided the tingling wasn't so bad now. He ought to be able to walk on it comfortably enough. He bent and reached down to take hold of his saddle.

"My, oh, my," he mumbled to himself. "What do we have here?"

A horse and rider appeared in the brush on the far side of the Rio Grande. The rider kept a tight rein on the animal and eased it out into the open slowly, the horse tossing its head as it tried to pull against the bit, but the rider wanting to take his time looking upstream and down instead of just stepping right out and into the water.

He sat on the bank there for a minute or more, then gave the horse its head and went into the river.

Billy was sure he'd seen that horse before, and as horse and rider came closer, he remembered where. The horse had a white stocking on the off fore and a patch on its rump that was probably a botched brand from a long time ago. The rider, wearing a blue bandanna and big hat, was the same fellow who'd been in the lead of those cow thieves.

Billy looked on the far bank behind him, but this time could see no suggestion there were other riders in the brush there, nor could he see any dust to hint of another bunch of stolen livestock.

Far as he could see, this time the rider was alone.

As far as he could see. Which didn't mean all that much. A thousand cows and a dozen circus elephants could be hidden over there, and Billy none the wiser until they decided to show themselves.

He eased his saddle back down onto the ground and picked up the Marlin carbine instead. He tried to remember if he'd already levered a cartridge into the chamber, or if he ought to take care of that little detail now while the rider was too far away to hear the oiled steel lever action clatter.

His heart began to pump hard and loud.

"IS anybody there?" The cowboy brought his horse to a halt about twenty, thirty yards out from the mesquite tree where Billy made his spy nest. "Don't shoot, mister. I'm just riding by."

Billy wasn't sure what he ought to do. The young cowboy did seem to be alone. And he was keeping his hands well clear of the pistol strapped to his leg. Almost certainly, Billy saw, the revolver would have to be latched into the leather somehow for it to be carried at that angle. Just like Mr. Adler warned him about. The good thing

about that was that if that was true, it showed the cowboy
wasn't interested in getting his gun out.

"Are you there, mister?"

Billy grunted. And stepped out into the open with his
carbine cradled across his chest, his right hand on the grip
and thumb draped over the hammer. He thought—was
pretty sure really—that he had a cartridge in the chamber
but the hammer down. He could drag the hammer back and
get his carbine into action a lot quicker than the fellow on
the horse over there could unfasten his revolver and pull it
out.

The idea of two thoroughly inept young gunfighters
having at each other and neither of them knowing how to
go about it struck Billy's funny bone, and he began to grin.
"Hello," he called. "Step down if you like and join me. I
got a leftover chicken leg if you'd like. Nothing but water
to drink, though."

The cowboy dismounted and dropped his rein ends to
the ground.

"You trust that horse to ground-tie like that?" Billy
asked.

"Sure I do."

"Back where I come from, do you know what they call
a man who teaches his horse to ground-tie?" Billy asked.

"What's that?"

"A pedestrian."

The cowboy laughed and came forward to shake hands.
"Jim Tibbett is my name."

Billy introduced himself.

"Maybe where you come from," Tibbett said, "the fellows don't have to worry so much about getting a horse

moving all that quick. Ground-tying can be a big help if you're in a hurry."

"Lucky for me I've never been in all that big a hurry, I guess," Billy said.

"Lucky for you," Tibbett repeated. He nodded toward Billy's shirt. "That's not a Ranger badge, and there's no other lawdogs around here. Least I never thought there were."

"I'm Federal," Billy told him. "Mounted Patrol." Which sounded ever so much better than to say he was a Chinese Immigration Agent, he thought.

"Federal? Damn. You gonna be here a while?"

"For a while, yeah."

"You could've shot somebody yesterday."

"I didn't want to," Billy admitted. "Didn't see there was any call for that."

"I appreciate that, Patrolman Billy."

Tibbett paused, then said, "You know . . . not that I'm admitting to anything, mind . . . but if . . . just say 'if' . . . if a cow was to get itself stole from over on the Mex side and brought over here and sold to honest folks, well, it wouldn't be no white man got hurt by it."

"No, I expect there wouldn't. How about when some Mexican comes over and steals himself some cows right back?"

Tibbett chuckled. "Then I expect he'd be a low-down sneaky son of a bitch of a thieving Mexican, wouldn't he?"

"Could be better all the way around if both sides left be," Billy suggested.

"That's a thought, all right."

"You want that chicken leg, Jim? It won't be any good

time I carry it all the way back to town in this heat. I think I may have most of a biscuit to go with it."

"Bring you a lunch and just set up your office out here, do you?"

"Yes, I do." Billy picked up the brown-paper bundle his lunch had been put up in and handed it to Tibbett.

"Thanks." Jim hunkered down and ate what was left from Billy's lunch. From this angle, Billy could see there was a retaining thong holding Jim's Colt in place.

Billy felt kind of silly to be standing there holding his carbine ready, so he set the gun butt down against the bole of the mesquite and picked up his canteen. He took a swallow, then offered the water to Jim, who also had some.

"That's good, thanks."

"Any time," Billy told him.

"As lawmen go," Jim said, "you're all right."

"I suppose I could say the same about you, except you're the first outlaw I've ever met. Social-like, that is."

"Aw, some of us are damn near human," Jim said with a grin.

The cow thief stood and dusted the seat of his britches with both hands, then carefully wiped his right palm along his trousers to get the chicken grease off before extending his hand to Billy again. "I'm glad we got to meet," he said. "Thanks for the grub, Patrolman Billy."

"Drop by again any time, Jim. I expect I'll be here for a spell."

Tibbett paused for a moment, then smiled and nodded. "Take care of yourself, Billy."

"You too, Jim."

Tibbett went back to his horse and gathered his reins, then stepped onto the saddle. The horse hadn't moved half a yard in any direction since he'd dropped the reins. Billy was impressed. It really is damn near impossible to train a horse to ground-tie, but Jim Tibbett or somebody had sure managed it with this animal.

Tibbett touched the brim of his hat and smiled, then wheeled his horse back in the direction of the Rio Grande and Mexico.

Billy liked the young rider, who did not appear to be any older than he was and maybe not yet even that old.

He liked Jim. But in a way he hoped he never saw him again.

"You take care," he said half under his breath. Then once again picked up his saddle and got ready to head back to town.

THIRTY-SEVEN

Dearest Billy;

It is my ernest wish that this finds you in best health despite the dangers of your job. I must admit that I am exceeding proud of you, my dear Billy. You are honest and desent and very handsome too. I count myself a fortunate woman to have your esteem.

Rec'd yr letter written upon the train and have tried to find this Marly in the atlas at the school, but it is not shown so I can only imagine where it must be. Wherever it is, dear Billy, so my thoughts are too.

We had a rain last week which quite annoyed papa as he just finished mowing hay and he feared it would sour, but now says he can rake and turn it and it should cure properly.

Saw your mama at services on Sabbath last. I assured her you are well, but as promised did not give her particulars. She cried so that I was sorely tempted to elaborate, but could not bring myself to break my promise made to you.

Jason and me have gathered prickly pear blossoms and our mama is putting up preserves of them.

Johnny Coyle has come by several evenings of late, but I remind him that I am spoken for and well pleased to be so.

Charlie Bent took a tumble, he says, when his horse bucked, but I heard he was in his cups and just fell off. He broke his arm and banged his head, but he will be all right.

Billy dearest, I think of you every day and miss you. I will write to you again soon.

With fond regards and warmest affection I am,
Edith

THIRTY-EIGHT

BILLY'S chest swelled with pride and joy. He stood on the walk in front of the saloon where they lived—he had not written anything to Edith about that sordid little detail nor had he mentioned to her the rather notorious identity of his partner—and read her letter for the third time.

Edie was still his. And Johnny Coyle better watch himself or the next time they met, Billy was going to bust him one. Johnny was two years older and twenty pounds heavier, and he'd better watch his step or Billy would bust him but good. Dang him.

He could see Edie's dear face just as clear as if she were standing before him. The thought of her, the imagined sight of her, made him tremble, and he knew he would have trouble getting to sleep tonight for thinking about her.

He glanced every so often at the traffic going past, mostly folks on foot coming from or headed toward the bridge across to the Mexican side. Heavy traffic, horses and wagons and the like, had to use the ferry that crossed just above the bridge or the very busy ford two miles to the north, so it was rare to see horses on this block. Billy glanced up at the approach of three horses.

A welcoming smile spread across his face when he recognized Mr. Adler riding the first animal in line.

Then the smile was wiped away when he saw the other two were being led. And the burdens they carried.

The second horse in line was one he recognized from . . . what was it? Three days ago when he'd shared his lunch with an outlaw? He'd gotten a good close look at it then. And again now. The horse had a white stocking on the one foreleg.

And the dead man draped across its saddle wore a blue bandanna.

"Oh, no!"

As the veteran lawman and gunfighter came closer, Billy could see that the man carried on the second horse was dark-skinned. Probably Mexican. He must have been the fourth rider when they crossed at the south ford.

Tibbett had come by, Billy realized now, to determine if that ford south of town was still being watched. Because Billy was keeping guard there, Jim and his friends must have tried to slip a stolen herd across at one of the upstream fords.

Now Jim Tibbett was dead and one of his partners too.

Billy felt sick to his stomach.

"THEY didn't give me any choice," Tuck Adler said over a cup of whiskey. "I waited until they were across, of course, to make everything legal. Then I stepped out to demand they show some papers on the cows or give themselves over to the law.

"Before I had a chance to say anything, the young white boy pulled his pistol and took his chances. I shot him first, then the Meskin. The other three hightailed it back over to the Mex side. Once they turned and started the other way, I let them go. Could have dropped at least one more and maybe two, but there wasn't any need for that. They were running and presented no danger.

"The cows wheeled around and started after the thieves, back into Mexico. I let them go too, of course. Maybe they'll head back to whatever ranch they were stolen from."

Billy realized that Mr. Adler might know an awful lot about fighting and such, but he wasn't so well versed when it came to livestock. A horse can be pretty much counted on to head for home if it's turned loose. And a milk cow that is barn-fed might, just might, come back to its barn if it gets lost. But an ordinary range beeve will wander from shade to grass and on to the next patch without any regard for where its drifting takes it. A steer can turn up a hundred miles from its home range if it isn't contained somehow, especially if it is moving along with a storm at its back.

Adler went on. "There must have been sixty, seventy head in the herd. And an extra rider from when you saw them before. They must have been trying to make up for losing that bunch the other day." He shrugged. "Some people learn. Others get themselves dead before they learn anything."

"Jim was a nice fella," Billy said. He wasn't sure why he felt called upon to defend Tibbett. But he had liked the young outlaw. That's really what it came down to. Billy had just plain liked him.

"That may be, but he made his last mistake when he tried to shoot me."

Billy sighed. "Yes, sir. I suppose he did."

"Come on now. No need to look so glum. Why, it could be there's rewards posted for your friend or that thieving Meskin. If there is, you and me will split it." He smiled. "You never know. We might turn up fifty dollars or so on them."

Blood money, Billy thought.

Then he decided he was being silly. There was nothing wrong with the law posting reward money for the capture of criminals. And Jim had been a criminal. Dammit, he had.

This business of wearing a badge wasn't as easy as Billy'd thought it would be.

He intended to write to Edie again tonight. But he wouldn't be telling her anything about Jim Tibbett or his demise.

"I need a refill here, boy. How's about I bring you a beer when I come back."

"Sure, I . . . no, could I have a whiskey instead, please?"

Adler laughed and clapped him on the shoulder. "Damn right, boy. Two whiskeys, coming up."

THIRTY-NINE

BILLY was drunk. He knew he was drunk. He liked it.

He had no worries. No cares. He laughed. He could not remember why he was laughing, but something must have been funny. So he laughed again at his own silliness for laughing when he couldn't remember why.

He reached for the whiskey bottle and tipped a generous tot into his mug, then drank it down. Oh, my, but that did taste good. Warm. It tasted warm. He hadn't known anything could *taste* warm. But this whiskey did. It went down as gentle and nice as whipped cream. But warm. Could you whip cream when it was warm? He didn't think so. That was all right. You didn't need to just so long as you had whiskey. Why hadn't he ever known how good whiskey is? 'Bout time he learned, that was for sure.

"Are you hungry, boy?"

Billy blinked. He was having a little trouble getting his

eyes to focus. Over there. Mr. Adler was over there. On the other side of the table. It was a long way to the other side of the table. Long way.

"I asked, are you hungry?"

Billy nodded.

He looked across the table at Mr. Adler. Or tried to. Mr. Adler wasn't there. Now that was an amazing trick. One second Mr. Adler was there. The next moment he wasn't. Wonderful. Billy wondered how he'd done that. Maybe someday he would teach Billy that trick. They were partners, weren't they? Surely he would teach Billy how to disappear like that.

Mr. Adler wasn't there, but the whiskey bottle was. Billy upended it over his cup, spilling a little but getting most of it out so he could drink it. Which he did.

"Here y' go, kid."

Billy jumped a little, startled. There was that trick again. There. Not there. Now he was there again. It was marvelous.

A rich aroma of chilies and stewed beans rose off the bowl Mr. Adler put in front of him. It was the most wonderful smell he'd ever smelled. Ever. The scent made his mouth water and his belly ache. He took hold of the spoon sticking out of the red and brown mass of beans and managed to get it to his mouth. The beans tasted even better than they smelled.

Not as good as the whiskey, though. Nothing tasted as good as the whiskey did. Billy picked up his cup and tried to drink from it, but the damn thing was empty. He reached for the bottle, but it was empty too. He shook it. Looked inside. Damn thing was empty, all right. He threw it onto the floor.

"Still thirsty, kid? That's fine. I'll bring us another."

Mr. Adler was gone. In the blink of an eye. There. Gone. There again. Gone again. Fantastic.

Billy had some beans. Drank some whiskey.

Now where the hell did that whiskey come from? He glared at the floor as if it offended him. The empty whiskey bottle was right there where he'd put it. But now there was another bottle on the table. And Mr. Adler was back. Amazing. Billy really loved that trick Mr. Adler did.

"Have another drink, kid."

He did. And some more beans. Lordy, those were good beans. Best damn beans he ever put a lip on.

He picked up his mug. Spilled just a little of the whiskey. Drank down the rest. Oh, my. It was good. Better even than the beans.

Billy looked at Mr. Adler and began to laugh.

FORTY

OH, God!

He wasn't blaspheming. He was genuinely appealing to the Father. For . . . almost any sort of help. He needed so much help that he couldn't begin to know where to start in on the asking.

He felt . . . awful. Just awful. His head hurt. And the side of his face. And his knees. And his tongue. His tongue tasted vile. Even worse than the rest of the inside of his mouth. His mouth tasted kind of like the pit under a privy smelled.

Last night . . . he couldn't remember much of last night. Not after a certain point, he couldn't.

He had bits and snatches of recollection. A picture drawn here. Another one there. They didn't necessarily connect one to another.

One was a face. A young girl's face. Mexican, maybe.

Not pretty, though. This face was flat and swarthy, and the girl had bad teeth. Why he would conjure up an image like that when he could just as easily think about a pretty girl . . . he did not know.

Another picture in his mind was like a regular picture except this picture moved. His mind held two or three seconds of this picture that moved. He was in the courtyard between the saloon and his room. He was on his knees. He was puking. The beans and whiskey tasted terrible. Like the inside of his mouth did now.

A picture came to him that caused him acute embarrassment. It was a woman's naked breast. He was uncomfortable now to find himself thinking about that.

Billy had seen breasts before. A number of times. When women were nursing their babies. There was nothing lewd about that, although of course a man pretended not to see, and honestly tried not to see, but of course sometimes you did see. That was all right. That was a pure and natural thing anyway.

But this . . . there wasn't any baby in this picture in Billy's mind. And it wasn't for any pure and decent cause that this breast was on display. He was not exactly sure how he knew that, but he was positive that this was so.

There was that brief image of a breast. Rounded. Melon-shaped. With a very dark, very large nipple set atop a brown mound of flesh.

And then, now that he thought about it, the image expanded. A soft, rounded belly. Black, curly patch of hair. And the sharp odor of sweat. Now why . . .

Billy gasped. His eyes came open and he lay rigid and unhappy on the narrow bed.

He was not alone on the bed. And the images from last night were no mere imaginings.

There was a dark-haired Mexican girl lying next to him. She had a flat, unlovely face, and her breath was sour.

The blanket that covered the two of them was pushed down to waist level on her side, and he could see all too clearly that she was indeed naked.

A skim of mucus dried white and scaly lay in the corner of her mouth, and there was a booger on the rim of her left nostril. She had pimples. Not just on her face either.

Billy felt like screaming.

He hadn't . . . oh, God . . . he couldn't have. . . .

He felt cold and empty. And unclean.

Dear Lord. What if this girl was diseased. *What had he done?*

Billy felt like crying. Damn this stuff about being a man grown. He wanted to cry. He really did.

He got up, discovered that he was naked too, and reached for his trousers. He had to go to the privy. He wanted to puke again.

What he really wanted right now was to die.

He dragged his britches on and, barefoot, lurched across the small room to the door with all the fervor of a man trying to escape the implacable hounds of Hell.

FORTY-ONE

Dear Miss Forester:

It is with a heavy heart that I take pen in hand this day.

I have pondered upon the future at great length and have come to the unhappy conclusion, Miss Forester, than I must break off communication with you.

It would serve no purpose to elaborate the several reasons why I conclude the necessity of this decision, save to say that I am not a worthy suitor for so good and decent a person as yourself.

I shall not burden you again.

Please know that you will forever be locked within my heart and mind as the fairest damsel of all.

My sorrow and my apologies are extended to you. I

know you will find someone worthy of you. That is my remaining hope.

In sadness and with respect, I remain
Truly yrs
William Delisle

FORTY-TWO

"BOY, you been moping around here for two days, acting like an old hound dog with a bellyache. I haven't seen you smile one time since the night you got taken drunk. You can't still be feeling bad from that. Hell, of course you aren't. You're eating again. If you can eat all this greasy Meskin cooking, you're just fine. Tell you what, though. You need cheering up. How's about I get us another bottle and you and me will tie one on."

Billy glared at him.

The letter was in the mail and on its way to New Mexico now. It was too late to change his mind even if he wanted to. Which he did not. All right, he did. He desperately wanted to call that letter back. And just as firmly he knew he would not even if he could.

He was a low, vile, utterly worthless piece of trash. The

sweetest, most beautiful girl in the world trusted him. Relied upon him. Loved him.

How did he treat her? He got drunk and took that girl to bed. A common trollop. He did not even know her name, for Pete's sake. Yet he bedded her. The shame of it burned in him.

He could not possibly present himself to Edith Jane now. Why, for all he knew that Mexican girl could have been diseased. He might . . . he did not know about such things. But all the fellows knew that women of the night often carry diseases. He could well have caught something from her. He could pass a disease on to Edith.

How would she like that? Catch a disease from her own husband? God, that would be awful. It would be criminal.

Except . . . he would never take dear and innocent Edith into a wedding bed.

Not now. He couldn't.

He had shamed himself. He did not deserve her. She was worthy of a decent and upstanding husband. Which he could never be.

He squeezed his eyes tight shut, willing himself to not cry again. Not here in public. Not here in the damned saloon. Alone in his room, that was a different situation. He had cried there. Tears were unmanly. But then Billy had already proven himself less than a man. A man is capable of exhibiting self-restraint. A man does not get drunk and wake up with a strange tart at his side.

Good God! He did not even know her *name*.

What sort of man would do a vile thing like that? A male who was no man, that was who.

"Do you want that last tortilla, boy?"

"No, sir."

Adler tore the tortilla into pieces and used them to sop up the bean juice in the bottom of his bowl.

Mr. Adler, the great and famous Tuck Adler, was totally unconcerned about things like drunkenness and debauchery. He could play cards and drink and bed the doxies—indeed did do exactly those things—night after night after night and never show the faintest signs of discomfort. Not physical nor emotional. He seemed to simply not care.

These past few days, Billy was sometimes tempted to harshly judge Mr. Adler.

In a way, he very much wanted to place the blame on the older man.

But it was not Mr. Adler who swallowed those drinks. Nor he who woke up with a stranger lying naked at his side.

The only person who was truly responsible for what was done was William Anders Delisle. No one else.

"You sure you don't want to share a bottle with me tonight, boy?"

"No. Thank you," Billy said stiffly.

"Yeah, well, whatever. Pass me that pepper sauce, will you?"

Billy excused himself and fled to the solitude of his room.

Edith. She deserved so much better than he had proven himself to be.

He closed the door and latched it and sat in the evening gloom not bothering to light the bedside lamp. His eyes became hot, and he felt the wet trickle of bitter tears roll down his cheeks.

FORTY-THREE

·

BILLY felt hot and sweaty and out of sorts as he rode back into town after another day uselessly wasted setting in the thin shade of a mesquite tree. He had not seen a Chinaman since they came to Marly, and hadn't even seen any rustlers making the crossing since Jim Tibbett's bunch more than a week ago.

Once or twice a day he would see a handful of Mexicans wade across on foot. Coming over to look for work, he supposed, or going home to their families with wages earned on the U.S. side. There was nothing illegal about that regardless of which direction they were traveling, and he doubted any of them so much as noticed there was Mounted Agent keeping watch over the ford. If any of them did see him, they gave no outward indication of it.

He was beginning to wonder why Mr. Adler insisted they stay here at the Marly fords. If there were a few thieves crossing, so what? Cow thieves weren't their business. Chinamen were. If the county sheriff or Texas Rangers wanted the cow thieves stopped, they were welcome to come do it themselves. Mr. Adler and Billy were not drawing seventy-five dollars a month from the United States government to do someone else's job.

If, that is, they ever actually collected their seventy-five and keep. So far Mr. Adler was paying for everything, either with the vouchers the major had given him back in El Paso or out of his own pocket. Mr. Adler always seemed to have plenty of money to spend. Probably from playing cards, which he did nearly every night.

The man was generous with his own money, buying Billy his rifle and ammunition and drinks and food . . . and paying for that flat-faced girl too, Billy supposed. He certainly hadn't had any money of his own to give her that horrible night. Mr. Adler must have paid her, thinking to do his partner a kindness. Never mind that it ruined Billy's life. It was surely intended as a kindness.

Billy did wish they would move along, though. Find some other spot where maybe for once they would spot an actual Chinaman and get to chase the poor son of a bitch back over into Mexico.

He rode slowly down the main street that terminated at the bridge over into Mexico, then dismounted and put the gray up for the night. He gave it a good rubdown and cleaned its hoofs and made sure it had bright, mold-free hay to eat and fresh water in the trough.

He did not see Mr. Adler's horse in the stable. Not that there was anything unusual about that. Sometimes Mr. Adler would stay out for several days, God knows doing what. Probably he was over on the Mexican side drinking and playing cards, Billy guessed. He did not ask, and Mr. Adler never said.

Billy went around to the street and into the saloon. He was hungry and wanted to get supper over with early so he could ask for a tub and some water to be brought to his room. At the government's expense. Normally he would have gone down to the barbershop for a bath, but you had to have cash money to pay for that, and Billy didn't have so much as a copper halfpenny to his name. The bath, like his supper, would have to go on the expense voucher they were holding at the saloon.

"Hello, Mr. Nelson."

"Evenin', Billy. You look tired."

"Yes, sir, a little. Could you have a tub and some water sent to my room after I eat, please?"

"I can do that. It will be there waiting for you. Do you want to eat now or would you have a drink first?"

"I'd like some supper, please. Just water to drink." He did not trust himself after that last experience with alcohol.

"Go ahead and pick a table. I'll have Carmen bring your food."

"Thank you, sir."

Billy was halfway across the crowded room when he heard, "Oh, wait a moment. Hey! Billy. Billy Delisle."

He turned and saw Mr. Nelson holding an envelope overhead. "I forgot. This came for you today."

Billy felt like all the blood drained clean away from his head. He was shaky on his legs when he went back over to the bar and accepted the letter. He knew from the handwriting who'd written it. He thought he might throw up.

He felt a little better—not much, but a little—after he looked more closely and saw from the postmark that the letter had to have been written before Edith received his last-ever note to her. The two had crossed in the mail.

Even so, it was a bitter thing now to receive a letter from her.

God, he loved her. He missed her. He wished . . .

A man seated off at the side of the busy, happy saloon rose and dropped his hat onto the table before him.

"You," he said in a loud, strong voice. "You're Billy Delisle?"

"Yes, I am. I . . ." Billy stopped, his mouth locked open, when he realized where he had seen this man before.

This was the middle-aged white man who had been riding with Jim Tibbett that day they brought the stolen cows across.

Billy tried feverishly to remember everything Mr. Adler had tried to teach him about facing a man with a gun.

Grab iron fast. Never mind taking aim. Shoot fast. Two quick shots to rattle the other man. Then bear down and place the third round once the other man was already shaking.

Oh, Jeez! Billy's mouth was dry and his palms sweaty.

He very carefully transferred Edith's letter into his left hand, folded it, and stuffed it into his shirt pocket. For some reason, it seemed important to him that he not drop that letter.

"I believe you knew my son Jimmy Tibbett," the man with the graying hair said.

"Yes, sir. Yes, I did."

The other patrons in the saloon scattered like two coveys of quail, one bunch flapping to either side so there was a wide aisle in the middle with only Tibbett and Billy standing facing each other.

Billy wasn't sure whether he would be shot first.

Or fall down in a faint.

He flexed his fingers and wiped his right hand against his shirtfront in an effort to dry it.

Mentally, he was rehearsing the movements he needed to make in order to grab the butt of his Smith and Wesson and bring it into line.

He felt shaky and weak. *I do not want to do this,* he was telling himself. *I do not.*

FORTY-FOUR

"I came to get Jimmy's body," Tibbett said, his voice conversational rather than challenging. "Jimmy liked you, y'know. He never suspected you would play him false like you did."

Billy had no idea what Tibbett meant when he said that last, but a wave of giddy relief flooded through him when he realized the man had not come here seeking revenge. "I never. . . ."

"I told him you can't trust any man who wears a badge, but he liked you. Now he's dead."

"I am truly sorry, Mr. Tibbett. I want you to know that."

"What I know, Billy Delisle, is that I am going to make trouble for you like you wouldn't believe. The governor is going to hear about what's going on down here. So are the Texas Rangers. I am going to have your badge and that old man's who's with you. You're going to be called to account for what you did to my boy, Billy Delisle. You are going to pay for your murders."

Tibbett reached down.

Billy thought he intended only to pick up the hat he'd put on the table. It did not look to him that Tibbett was reaching for his revolver.

Behind Billy, from the doorway, a shot rang out and quickly another.

Tibbett blanched and froze in place, the fingers of his right hand touching the crown of his Stetson.

A third gunshot reverberated through the crowded room, and a dark spot appeared on the front of Tibbett's shirt.

Billy knew before he looked who was doing the shooting, who had to be there in the doorway.

Tuck Adler took his time with an aimed fourth shot. Billy watched in horror as Adler leveled his Colt, aimed, carefully squeezed off a finishing round.

Billy jerked his head around in time to see Tibbett fall, a bullet in his brain. A look of . . . it took Billy a moment to figure it out . . . contempt. A look of contempt was on the dead man's face. Or maybe that was only the result of distortion caused by the impact of Mr. Adler's .45 bullet.

"He was only. . . ." Billy clamped his mouth tight shut. It was too late now to protest that Tibbett wanted only to pick up his hat.

How could he be sure of that anyway? Mr. Adler knew far more about these things than Billy ever would. Or ever wanted to.

"Lucky I got here when I did," Adler said as he strolled over beside Billy, his fingers already busy with the almost unconscious task of ejecting his empties onto the saloon floor and reloading the Colt with fresh rounds. "He had you mesmerized, boy. Like a snake fixing to eat a chicken. You'd've just stood there and taken a slug in the belly if that man had his way." Adler finished reloading, flipped the cartridge gate shut, and slid his right-hand gun back into the holster under his armpit.

"Lucky I come in when I did, isn't it?" Adler asked.

Billy did not answer. He was staring at the dead man whose blood was seeping into the sawdust on the saloon floor.

There was an awful lot of blood to be soaked up. A terrible amount.

FORTY-FIVE

IT was several hours later, alone in his room, when Billy remembered the letter from Edith. He turned the lamp wick high and got the letter from his pocket, then sat with it on his lap for agonizing minutes more before finally—and very, very carefully—he slit it open and pulled out the two sheets of composition pad paper inside.

Dearest Billy:

I am so excited, dear Billy. I wish you were here so I could tell you my news in person. And for more reasons than just being able to tell you. But I am sure you know what I mean when I say that.

Am I being too forward, my dear? Am I being lewd? Please do not hate me. It is just that I LOVE YOU, BILLY DELISLE.

There! I said it. Right there in plain words.

I love you.

*And I commit my feelings to paper without shame
or reticence.*

*I can do that, Billy. Do you know why? We have my
parents' blessing. Really.*

*This morning my father had to go to town. My
mother had him bring back for me a small but very
sturdy cedar chest, an entire bolt of good cloth, and a
pair of candleholders. Do you know why? She said
you will surely be coming home soon and that it is
time I begin putting together my Hope Chest. She said
I should begin by sewing a shirt for you, Billy. She
said the first thing into my chest should be for you.
Just as my first thoughts in the morning and my last at
night should be for you.*

*Oh, Billy. My thoughts are of you. Morning and
night and all the time between. And in my dreams as
well, ha ha.*

*You have no sisters and so you may not know how
very much a Hope Chest means between a mother and
her daughter. And her advice. It means a lot to me.
You mean everything to me.*

I LOVE YOU, BILLY DELISLE! ! !

I do.

*I look forward to using that very small but so very
meaningful phrase again.*

Very soon, I hope.

*When you come home, Billy, I will have your shirt
sewn and folded and waiting in my cedar Hope Chest.*

*With all my love, dearest Billy,
YOUR Edith*

It was a long time again that night before he could sleep, and then it was only exhaustion that gave him a brief period of fitful rest.

FORTY-SIX

IT never rains in south Texas? Ha! Now wasn't that a lie. This was about as lousy a day as Billy could remember. A wall of cloud had moved in from the east, from out where there was supposed to be a bunch of water in the Gulf of Mexico. Well, a lot of that water had come inland, apparently for the sole purpose of making Billy Delisle's life even more miserable than it already was.

It was one of those hard, steady, all-day-soaker sort of rains. Back in New Mexico—it was still hard to avoid thinking of New Mexico as home—everybody would be happy with a rain like this one. The graze and the gardens would flourish after a rain like this.

Down here . . . he looked around. Maybe the mesquite and prickly pear and the few sprigs of dry, wiry bunchgrass would like it.

He had borrowed a square of canvas tarp and rigged

himself a shelter, but even so he was mostly wet and clammy, and a trickle of cold water kept finding its way off the brim of his hat and onto his lower back, then down inside his belt and onto his backside. That ought to be chilled enough by now that he could just sit on the churn and turn himself a batch of ice cream. If he had a churn. And the makings for ice cream, whatever those were.

He sighed. There was probably no reason to be out here anyway. Come the end of the day, the Rio Grande would be swollen to the point that no one could cross over at the fords anyhow. He probably should have laid up in bed today.

But if he did that, dammit, he would only wind up thinking too much.

Which he was doing out here anyway, the only difference being that back in his room he could be miserable in comfort. Here he had the cold and the wet to go with his other miseries.

He'd made a mess of everything, he thought morosely. A thoroughgoing, full-blast, double-run, damn-all mess.

But if you're going to do something, you might as well do it right. Right?

Somehow remembering his father's frequently repeated admonishment did not make him feel a damn bit better, even though he had certainly done a bang-up job of making a mess of his life.

He took a swallow of water from his canteen—he could as easily have taken a drink by tipping his head back under the edge of the canvas—and ate half the cheese sandwich that was in the bag lunch they'd put up for him back at the saloon.

Billy wondered if Mr. Adler had bothered going out

today. He'd still been asleep when Billy rode out this morning. Probably sleeping off the effects of last night. For the next couple days, Billy thought, he would lay out himself. Just stay in his room and feel sorry for himself.

Now there was a fine idea, he grumbled silently to himself. Why, he . . .

Whoa! His head came up and he rose into a crouch so he could see more clearly.

It was hard to tell, what with the rain and a bit of mist hanging over the river, but over on the far side there . . .

Be damned!

Bad as this weather was, somebody was out moving in it.

Somebody, he thought, who was probably counting on there not being anybody watching the ford on a day like this.

Somebody who was willing to bet he could still make it across before the water got too high.

Whoever it was, Billy hoped he was right about being able to cross. Drowning was a mighty harsh penalty for being wrong about something like that.

A figure on foot, but wearing a horsebacker's yellow slicker, came out into the open. The slicker looked odd on a man afoot since it had the extra oilskin at the back where it was intended to fit over the cantle of a saddle too.

The man in the slicker walked to the bank and looked things over, then turned and beckoned. He was joined by four . . . no, five . . . dark shapes. These had no rain gear and were bundled deep into their regular clothes. They were bound to be wet and cold. But then they would be regardless once they got into that rising, swift-moving water.

Even after seeing those people on foot, Billy half-expected to also see a clutch of cows come out of the brush. On a day like this, law-abiding Mexicans or Americans either one could be expected to walk on up to Marly and cross on the bridge there rather than risk the water.

Which, he realized, suggested that there was something about this bunch that was not law-abiding.

He watched from beneath his crude shelter as first the one in the slicker, and then the other five, stepped gingerly into the water and began forging through the increasingly turbulent Rio Grande.

FORTY-SEVEN

OH, Jesus!

He saw it first; then seconds afterward, the sound of the scream reached him through the heavy, rain-sodden air.

One of the people in the water lost his footing and was swept away from the others.

Billy was standing there watching somebody die.

Oh, God. No.

He ran for his horse and grabbed up his reins. Leaped for the saddle without taking time to find his stirrup.

The gray jumped into a belly-down run without having to be spurred, and for a couple seconds there Billy was occupied down below with trying to find the damned stirrups and stuff his boot toes into them, while up higher he was fumbling with the saddle string that held his catch rope.

He yanked the rope loose and shook out a loop, guiding the gray with his knees as he did so.

He still hadn't managed to find the stirrups, which were flapping wildly as the horse ran.

The horse almost fell as it raced down the slope to the river's edge, and Billy almost came out of the saddle when it lurched. Both got themselves righted, and they thundered past the handful of bedraggled and frightened people who were just clambering onto the safety of solid ground on the Texas side.

Billy could see the man in the water now, floundering and splashing, dipping underneath the surface and then popping back up again.

The fellow was seventy, eighty yards downriver and moving with the current.

Billy raced well past the stricken man and hauled the gray to a sliding stop. It was going to be a helluva long throw out to where the man would float past. He finally managed to find his stirrups and stood in them, trying to assess the footing at the edge of the river.

The hell with it. He needed to get closer. He bumped the gray, and the horse delicately, reluctantly, tiptoed its way into the swiftly moving water.

When it was hock-deep, Billy stopped again and reined the horse just a little to his left to get a better angle. He figured he was going to get one good throw and maybe not another.

Back at the ranch, it hadn't mattered all that much if he missed a calf's heels. One throw of a rope didn't determine life and death back there.

Here . . .

He took a deep breath, shook out the rain-heavy manila, and made sure of his loop.

He stood as tall as he could get in the stirrups, gauged the speed of the drowning man as best he could, and . . .

Threw!

FORTY-EIGHT

THE loop opened wide and sailed high and long. Out over the water. Out over, perfectly, the head of the terrified fellow in the river.

Billy breathed again. He hadn't realized at the time that he was not breathing. Now he did.

He gulped for air and watched as the drowning man's flailing hands splashed down over the hemp. Billy took a quick wrap on the saddlehorn, and turned the gray hard left so its rump was facing the Rio Grande.

He felt the strain as the man in the water came up short against the rope.

Billy bumped the horse forward. It leaned into the task as if a steer were caught at the end of the rope, except this steer was light and easy to pull.

The gray stepped out of the river and up the bank, dragging the river's would-be victim with it until he lay on the muddy, rain-soaked earth. Billy left the rope affixed securely to his saddle lest by some awful accident the fellow slip back into the river. He dismounted and ran back to the fellow on the ground.

By then, the others who had safely gotten across were running to join him, the man in the slicker trailing behind.

Billy knelt beside the man he'd just rescued from drowning. He was still breathing. He was . . . .

Billy blinked. And stopped midway through the automatic task of stripping the rope off his catch.

The fellow who'd been drowning wasn't a fellow. It was a girl.

And she wasn't Mexican.

She was Chinese.

She was tiny. Young. Not much bigger than a newborn Hereford.

She coughed. Spat out some water. Struggled to sit upright.

Billy helped her into a sitting position and finished retrieving his rope.

The others who had crossed with her came stumbling up, gasping for breath and sliding on the muddy soil.

They were all Chinese, he saw, and all young women. All except for a white man who had the yellow slicker.

Chinese. Real damn Chinese. And an American to guide them across.

Illegally across, dammit.

Billy looked at the Chinese, who now were clustered close around him and the girl on the ground. They were chattering among themselves in their high-pitched, yip-yap language.

"What are they saying?" Billy asked their guide.

"Damn if I know. I don't talk none of that stuff. I just collect my five bucks a head an' lead 'em over."

"Where to?"

The man shrugged. "Fella meets me over there." He gestured vaguely toward the east. "He loads 'em into a wagon. I dunno where they go after that. Whores prob'ly. Or factory workers up north someplace. I dunno and it ain't any of my business anyhow. Come to think of it, why d'you care?"

Billy smiled and started coiling his rope so he could return it to its proper place on his saddle. "The reason I care," he said, "is that I'm a Federal officer, and I'm putting you and all five of them under arrest for illegal entry into the United States of America. So let's all rest up a bit, then we'll start walking up to Marly."

"Hey! You can't do that."

"I'm pretty sure that I can. But I'm afraid that I don't have any handcuffs or anything like that, so if you give me any trouble, about the only thing I'll be able to do is to shoot you. Now lift that slicker, please, so I can see if you're armed. Then I'll collect whatever weapons there are and we can get on our way."

Billy couldn't believe it. Chinese. Actual Chinamen. Well, Chinawomen.

Shee-oot!

FORTY-NINE

BILLY was proud as a peacock when he finally herded his covey of Chinese quail—and one very gloomy American fellow—into Marly. It was well past dark by then, thanks to the slow pace of his prisoners, and the truth was that he was not entirely sure what he should do with them now that he had them.

He wanted to dismount and take care of the gray. But he couldn't leave the prisoners standing in the street while he did so.

There was no jail in Marly, no local law that he could sign them over to. And he had no manacles or spancels or any of that prisoner-keeping stuff. Not that he would have been comfortable about chaining a bunch of young girls to a tree anyway. You could do that with a man, but not a girl. And a couple of the girls looked to be mighty young.

Barely into their teens, he was guessing. It was a quandary, and that was a fact.

He settled for motioning them underneath a porch overhang in front of the saloon. The rain had stopped, and they had all dried out fairly well on the march up from the ford, but the sky looked like it could start dripping again at any moment.

That was just his luck, he figured. Marly probably got rain once every two or three years. It would have been an dang awful lot more comfortable if the dang rain had held off for another six or eight months.

Even so, by golly, he had his prisoners. He'd found some Chinese. He was doing his job.

"Stay right there," he warned the American, who claimed his name was John Smith. Which, Billy supposed, it might actually have been, although he was a mite skeptical on that point.

He stepped over to the saloon door and peeped inside. Mr. Adler was sitting at a card table with a bottle on one side and a doxy on the other.

"Psst."

He tried again a little louder. "Yoo-hoo."

"Hey, dammit. Adler!"

That got his attention.

Billy motioned for him to come out. Adler scowled and hesitated for a moment, then he said something to the floozy and stood. He yawned and stretched, then ambled over to the doorway where Billy was waiting.

"What is it, boy?"

Billy grinned at him. And pointed.

"What the . . . well, I'll be a son of a bitch!" Adler came outside and stood for a moment marveling at the sight of the five quietly twittering Chinese girls and a rather sheepish John Smith.

"I caught them," Billy said. Which was probably unnecessary, but he announced it anyway.

"So I see."

"So now, uh . . . what should I do with them?"

"Oh, hell, just turn them loose, I suppose. Put 'em over the bridge back into Mexico."

"I can't do that."

"Why the hell not?"

"I've been thinking about that on the way up here, see. We have a chance to break up a whole ring of smugglers, Mr. Adler. Smith here, which he swears is his real name, Smith here says he brings them across the river and guides them to a spot about ten miles in from the border. The buyer meets him there and puts the girls into a closed wagon. He claims he doesn't know who the buyer is or where he takes the girls, but he says it's always girls that he brings over and probably they're being sold into slavery. Well, sort of slavery. He thinks they're forced into brothels someplace up north."

"Really?"

"That's what he told me. And what I was thinking, Mr. Adler, is that we could lock the girls up, then get Smith here to take us to meet the fellow who is buying girls and forcing them into that life. We could break the ring, don't you see, if we just get Smith to take us to meet the wagon."

"Thought that up all by yourself, did you?"

"It sounds good to me."

"You. Smith. You heard what he said. You'll take us to this wagon?"

"Yes, sir. Deputy Delisle said I could get a deal from the

court, maybe even get turned loose with no jail time, if I was to cooperate. Are you really Tuck Adler?"

"Yes, I am. Want to make something of it?"

"No, sir. I wouldn't cross you. No, sir."

Adler moved over to take a closer look at the girls. "Ugly damn things, aren't they?" he observed.

"I guess they don't have to be so pretty for what they do. Want to try one? Or two maybe? They aren't so bad in the dark," Smith said.

"Hush that kind of talk," Billy snapped. "We're officers of the law. You want to get charged with attempted bribery or something?"

"No. Sorry."

Adler looked annoyed for a moment, and seemed as if he were about to say something. Then he thought better of it and shrugged.

"What do you think, sir?" Billy asked him.

"I'll tell you. I think you have a pretty good plan, son. Except you didn't work it all the way out. Now I think about it, we can't turn these girls back into Mexico without somebody to take care of them. If they don't speak Mexican and they don't speak American that would be cruel, don't you think?"

"Yes, sir, I do."

"So what I think we should do, Billy, is that I'll have you shepherd these young women out to San Antonio. You'll find a courthouse there. Maybe even some Federal offices. You can turn these slant-eyed whores over to competent authority there, then come back here to join me.

"What I'll be doing in the meantime is taking Smith here out to meet this whoremaster with the wagon. I expect I can handle Smith and one or two fellows with that wagon. That way, just like you said, we'll break the ring. And we won't endanger these Chink bitches while we're doing it. Prob'ly oughtn't to make them walk all that way, I suppose, so we'll hire a wagon for you to carry them in. I expect you can make it there and back in ten or twelve days. While you're gone, I'll take care of Smith and his friend, then get back on post along the river down here."

"If that's what you think best," Billy said. He was disappointed at the idea he would not be there for the arrest of the fellow with the wagon. But then he wasn't here for his own glory; he was here to do a job, and he was proud to be able to do it.

"For tonight, we'll chain Smith to a post out in the barn and put the girls in one of the stalls. You and me can take turns watching them through the night. You look tired, Billy. I'll take the first watch while you get yourself some sleep."

"Yes, sir. Thank you."

Billy felt downright full of himself when he went to his room to change into clothes that hadn't been soaked for half the day and to get a few hours of rest before it was his turn to stand watch over the prisoners. His prisoners.

FIFTY

BILLY never did find out what any of their names were, but the Chinese girls were no trouble. They went wherever he pointed and did whatever he mimed they should do. The little one he'd pulled out of the river was so solicitous of him that it was embarrassing. Especially at night, when he had to forcibly evict her from his bedroll, and even then she insisted on sleeping curled tight against his feet.

He made fair time in the hired rig, an old ambulance with passenger benches in the back instead of the farm wagon he'd expected.

When they reached the highway that ran from San Antonio to Laredo, he stopped at Tilden, where they had a telegraph line. He sent a message off to Major Bolton, and two and a half days later when they got to San Antonio, there was a deputy U.S. marshal waiting there to take charge of the girls.

"You did fine here, Delisle," the marshal told him.

Billy was more than a little in awe of the deputy, and certainly was envious of him. The man was tall and handsome with fierce mustaches and a flat-crowned brown Stetson hat, and he looked powerful enough that he could step into a prizefighting ring with Gentleman Jim himself and not be under any handicap. Oh, he was a fine-looking specimen. He made Billy feel like a dowdy little half-grown cockerel next to this man's rooster. Receiving praise from a fine fellow like this deputy was mighty fine indeed.

"I'll take over from here," the marshal assured him. "I'll take these women back to El Paso, where your people are rounding up someone who speaks Chinese to interrogate them before we deport them."

"You aren't going to just shove them back into Mexico, are you?" Billy was thinking about Mr. Adler's plan for them. "They don't speak Spanish. I've had a couple fellas try to talk Mexican to them, and they didn't understand a word."

"It won't be up to me nor, for that matter, won't be up to you either, but my guess is that they'll be put on a ship back to China."

"That would be fine."

"There's a telegram waiting for you at the sheriff's office," the marshal said. "Your major is pleased with you, Delisle, and he's anxious to find out what your partner finds out from the American who was bringing these illegals in."

"That's nice."

"Could I ask you something, Agent Delisle? Confidential, so to speak?"

"Sure. Anything."

"Is it true that you're partnered with Tuck Adler?"

Billy grinned. "It sure is, Deputy. I've learned a lot from him."

The marshal scowled. He hesitated, then said, "You strike me as an honest man, Delisle."

"Lordy, I should hope so."

"Just be careful what-all you learn from that old sonuvabitch."

"Sir?"

"Never mind. It isn't my place to say anything. Here. I've wrote out a receipt for the prisoners. Soon as you sign my copy, they're officially off your hands, Agent."

"All right, sir. And . . . thanks."

The tall deputy nodded solemnly and made the exchange of signed receipts transferring the girls to his care.

FIFTY-ONE

BILLY found his way over to the Alamo, and this time walked alone through the sad, decaying ruins.

As a good New Mexican, he had no high regard for Texas or Texans. They were all blowhards and braggarts, as any New Mexico boy could tell you.

But as an American, he had to think of this as a special place. A place where freedom reigned. Where stout hearts and firm resolve stood against wrong, and even in defeat managed to prevail.

Under some slabs of rotting wood, he found a small and twisted scrap of lead and put it into his pocket. It might well have been lost there by some ten-year-old local kid with a slingshot. But it could as easily have been part of a musket ball fired by Jim Bowie or Davy Crockett or Colonel Travis.

Well, maybe not by Bowie. They said he was lying sick

inside one of the rooms somewhere when they came for him.

But it could have come from the gun of one of those other heroes. Billy liked to think maybe it had.

He stood inside the tumbledown old mission church for a few minutes—with his hat off, as Mr. Adler had admonished him the last time he was here—then went out and climbed onto the hired wagon.

It would be a four-day trip back to Marly, and he was eager to get there now.

For the first time since he'd pinned that badge to his shirt, he was feeling like he could make a difference by wearing it.

FIFTY-TWO

BILLY pulled his team to a halt and stood on the driving box. He wasn't sure if he should draw his revolver or not. But sure as anything, riding toward him on the road from Marly was the fellow who swore his name was John Smith.

Smith was mounted now and was carrying a gun of his own. When he saw Billy, he waved a casual hello and came to a stop close beside the wagon.

"What are you doing here?" Billy blurted. "I thought you'd be in jail."

"For what? It's legal for me to come and go across that river. I'm as American as you are."

Billy supposed that was true. But he didn't especially like it. He was flabbergasted when Smith added, "Anyways, I'm on your side now."

"My side?"

Smith winked at him. "Tuck will tell you all about it."
Billy frowned.

"Listen, I got things I need to do," Smith said, "so I'll
be riding on now. You take care, hear?" He bumped his
horse into motion and with another wave, put the animal
into a lope toward the east.

"DAMN if I know what he was talking about," Adler said
that evening over supper. "He was right that he hadn't broken any laws, none that I know about anyway, so I couldn't
hold him for anything. But . . . how did you put it? On our
side now?" He shrugged. "Beats me, boy. Maybe he meant
he's had a change of heart or something. Maybe because of
that girl almost drowning. That's about the only thing I can
think he might've meant."

"Yes, sir. Well, I suppose it isn't important anyhow. Oh!
I almost forgot." He searched through his pockets and
found the yellow telegraph form, now rather thoroughly
crumpled, he'd been given back in San Antonio. He was
smiling when he unfolded it and handed it to Adler. "The
major is mighty pleased with us."

"Now isn't that nice," the aging gunfighter said as he
read the congratulatory message. "Yes, it surely is. You did
good, Billy."

There it was. Mr. Adler called him by name again. That
didn't happen so very often, and it pleased him when it did.

"Are you ready to get back out on post now? Keep
watching for Chinamen? I know I'm ready for some help
after trying to cover all three fords by myself while you
were off seeing the city lights."

"You know I wasn't . . ."

Adler laughed. "I'm just funning you, boy. I know you're conscientious. Hell, you didn't have time to do much except drive up there, turn around, and come back."

"That's true."

"But tell me, Billy. Are those Chink girls as good as it's claimed? The night they were here, I didn't have time to try more than just the one. You must've got a better sample."

"Sir, I wouldn't do anything like that," Billy protested. He could feel his ears burn.

Adler's expression turned serious. "No, come to think of it, I bet you weren't interested at that."

Billy thought about protesting that it wasn't lack of interest that kept him from taking one of those poor, captive girls. The truth was that it had crossed his mind. What with his hope of marriage and a normal life being over now. But it just plain wouldn't have been right to do something like that to somebody that was powerless to resist. It wouldn't have been decent. He said nothing back to Mr. Adler, and concentrated on finishing his supper in silence after that.

FIFTY-THREE

My dearest Billy:

   My regard for you is unflagging. I love you. I do
not know what happened to cause you to reject me so
cruelly. Have you found another? Do you love her so
very much? I did not receive that impression from the
words you sent to me. I know that something dreadful
has happened. Did you kill a man in the performance
of your duties? Do you fear this would make a
difference in the way I feel toward you? Billy dearest,
nothing could make me love you less than I already
do. Than I have for so long. I have loved you, Billy
dear, since I was a child. I will always love you. If it is
your resolve that you will no longer care for me and
want to hold to your determination that I not become
your wife, that is a choice I cannot make for you,
although would that I could because I would bring

*you back into my arms without a moment's delay. If
you continue in this regard, Billy, it will make no
difference to me. I will wait here hoping always that
you will change your mind and you will come back to
me and you will let me hold you and feel you and kiss
you and be yours. Do you need me to be your woman,
Billy? I will be yours without marriage if that is your
desire, just tell me what you want me to do and I will
do it without fail because I love you, my Billy, I will
always love you and I will have no one if I cannot
have you. I will wait for you however long I must, if
that is to the end of my days, then that is how long I
will wait and I will be there waiting for you yet when
you reach the Great Reward above.*

*Come back to me, Billy. I will be here. Loving you.
Always.*

*Yours in faithful love,
Edith*

Billy wept.

He would have been tempted. No, he was tempted. But
for that signature.

Yours, she said. In "faithful" love.

Faithfulness was what he had failed to give her. And fi-
delity once broken can never be retrieved.

He sat alone in his room, Edith's letter in his hands, and
ached with the anguish that was in his heart.

FIFTY-FOUR

HE had forgotten how hot and itchy and boring it was to sit under that darned mesquite the whole day long. But then he hadn't found it so boring before. Then he'd been able to write long letters to Edith, or if not actually write, then think about what he would write the next time.

He could sit there and have imaginary conversations with her about everything he saw and everything he thought . . . and everything he hoped.

There had been so very much to hope for.

No longer. Now, just when it looked like things were going so well for him with this job, he had nothing to hope for.

The whole point of finding a good job had been to make enough money that he could marry Edith and take care of her. Now . . .

Even so, he realized, he was coming to like this business about being a Mounted Agent. He'd saved that Chinese girl from drowning. And he'd broken up a smuggling ring. Well, sort of broken it up. He supposed Mr. Adler was the one who really did that. After all, Billy only found the Chinese girls, and acted as a wagon driver to get them into the proper hands. Mr. Adler did everything else.

Billy frowned as something occurred to him. Mr. Adler told him that he'd arrested the ringleader and put him in manacles. He said that happened in a clearing in the thick, thorny brush they called the Brasada southwest of Tilden, where Billy had stopped to send his telegram to the major.

He found it curious that Mr. Adler hadn't sent a wire too. Surely the deputy marshal would have mentioned it if he had.

And come to think of it, why hadn't Billy passed Mr. Adler and his prisoner on the road?

There was only the one highway that ran from Tilden to San Antonio, and one would think Billy should have passed Mr. Adler somewhere along it on his way back to Marly. Unless he took the prisoner down to Laredo, of course.

That must be it then. He'd gone to Laredo. Billy hadn't known there were Federal authorities down there. But then there was an awful lot that he did not know.

He thought just out of curiosity, though, he would ask Mr. Adler about it that evening.

"NOT at all, boy. I don't mind a bit. Anything puzzles you, I want you to ask me about it. I've told you before. There's no secrets between partners. An' you and me are partners, right, kid?"

"Yes, sir, we surely are."

"Turning out to be a pretty damn good team too if I do say so," Adler told him.

"So what about that ringleader of the smugglers?" Billy asked. "How's come I didn't see you on the highway?"

"Because I wasn't on that road, boy. When I took him in, I went first to Tilden, just like you expected I should. I ran into a Texas Ranger at the courthouse there. A fella I've known for twenty years or more. Good man too. He said he had some business there, but he'd be glad to take the man off my hands and carry him in along with a coffle of prisoners of his own. If you didn't see him on the road he must not've been ready to head north before you already reached the turnoff and was on your way back here to Marly."

"Wouldn't the U.S. deputy marshal have said something to me about all that?" Billy asked.

"If he knew about it. I didn't send no telegram. I did write out a report and give it to my friend to deliver along with the prisoner so's they'd know who he was and what to do with him once he got to San Antone. I expect if the Ranger sent any telegrams, and I don't know did he or didn't he, he likely would've sent it to his own Ranger company, not to the U.S. marshal."

"Yeah, I can see how that would be so," Billy agreed.

"After supper," Adler said, "you want to have a few drinks with me? See what trouble we can get into?"

"No, sir. Thank you, but I'll just go out and get some air, I think. Walk down by the river and do a little thinking."

"Let me give you some advice, Billy, an' this comes from a man who's had more than his own fair share of living. There's no point in thinking too much. It only causes troubles. Leads to worry. And worry don't do a man any good at all. What you ought for to do is let the other fella fret over things. All you want to do, all I do, is have yourself a damn fine time of it. Play some cards. Pike a little monte. Have a few drinks. Lay a few doxies. Hell, boy, life is too short to waste any of it. Now loosen up and . . . say, you don't have any money for any of those things, do you. That's my fault, damn me. Here."

Adler reached into his pocket and brought out a handful of change that was heavy with yellow coins. He picked out a pair of ten-dollar eagles and three five-dollar coins and dropped them onto the table beside Billy's plate.

"This is no loan until payday now, boy. This is me taking care of my partner. Go on now. Don't be looking at me like that. Put those coins into your pocket and go have yourself some fun. Go on now or you'll hurt my feelings. Pick 'em up."

Billy didn't know what to say. It was one thing to accept a loan from Mr. Adler. But to take that much money as a gift? Mr. Adler didn't make any more money than Billy did. Well, except in his every-night card games, he supposed.

"Go on."

"Yes, sir. Thank you." Billy slipped the gleaming, heavy coins into his pocket. "Thank you, sir."

"The onliest thing I want in return is that you enjoy yourself some. You hear? Let your hair down, boy, an' enjoy life while you can because a man never knows how long he's got so you'd best make the most of it right here and now. That's my philosophy, Billy. Here and now. It's the only thing we can count on."

"Yes, sir. Thank you."

Adler left the table and headed toward the back of the saloon where the gambling and the girls were.

Billy figured he and Mr. Adler could discuss the difference between a gift and a loan come payday. Whenever that turned out to be.

He put his hat on and headed out into the cool of the evening. Wanting solitude. Wanting to forget. Knowing he would not.

FIFTY-FIVE

BILLY had a swallow of tepid water and wished the rain would come back. There was no wind moving, and the air lay hot and heavy over the cactus scrub that blanketed this end of Texas. It could get hot in New Mexico too, but he would have sworn that it never got this bad.

He took his hat off and let some of the air, what there was of it, reach his scalp, then set the hat loosely back in place.

He stood. Stretched. Belched. He'd finished his lunch a while ago, and wished he hadn't. It was too hot for food. The ham and cheese sandwich lay like a lump in his stomach, and if he had any sense at all he would quit putting more into his belly by drinking so often, but in this heat it was hard not to be thirsty.

Another hour, he figured, and the sun would be low

enough that he could start back to town without feeling like he was cheating on the job.

Over on the Mexican side of the river, there wasn't so much as a bird moving. Too hot and still for them too, he supposed.

Here on the Texas side . . . he blinked, then shaded his eyes and looked again. He could see something moving off to the southeast, downstream along the river. One . . . no, two distant objects. Definitely moving and, he thought, moving his way.

What he needed, he thought, was some of those binocular field glasses that made far-off things look closer. Billy had seen some of those in a store back in El Paso, but hadn't ever looked through them. When he could afford it—and when he could find some again—it would make sense to think about buying some of those. Or maybe he could ask the major about having field glasses issued to the Mounted Agents. It wouldn't hurt to ask surely.

The moving objects came nearer and ever nearer. He watched them for the better part of a half hour before he concluded that what he was looking at was hats. Pale-colored, wide-brimmed hats. Straw maybe. And the reason he was seeing just the hats was that whoever wore them was riding horseback so that the hats were visible above the low-growing scrub.

Eventually, as they came closer in among the scattered, patchy brush, he could make out the upper parts of the riders and then get glimpses now and then of the horses too.

There were two of them, and gradually they resolved themselves into a pair of men wearing white shirts, dark vests, and light-gray hats. Not straw. Just pale. They likely weren't working hands in that case, because a fancy hat like that would look plenty bedraggled and nasty the first time a calf got the squirts and sprayed watery crap all over the cowboy who was trying to tie or clip or brand it.

The riders weren't cow thieves either, at least not moving any stock with them right now, or Billy could have seen. Besides, even a small bunch of cows will raise a fair amount of dust.

They approached the ford Billy was watching, and one of them dismounted and seemed to be checking the ground there. Looking for tracks? Billy thought probably so.

The one who'd gotten off his horse mounted again, and left his partner there by the river while he put his horse into a trot upstream along the bank.

When he was a couple hundred yards north, he turned and waved to his partner, and then the both of them started riding away from the river.

Each of them rode just further from the water than Billy's hiding spot was.

Then turned in toward him. Both of them.

Whoever they were, they must have spotted him.

And they had him boxed, as tidy as if he was a steer that had been run into a squeeze chute.

"Oh, Lordy!" Billy mumbled.

He checked to make sure his .44 Smith lay loose in its holster, then looked to see that his carbine had a cartridge in the chamber.

He didn't cock the carbine. But he draped his thumb over the hammer so it was ready.

Cussing a little under his breath, he stepped out from under the mesquite so the riders would be able to see that he was armed and ready, just in case trouble was what they had in mind here.

FIFTY-SIX

THERE was no way he could keep close watch on both of them, what with them separating and coming toward him from two different directions, so Billy moved sideways to put the mesquite between himself and the one he judged to be further away. He stood facing the other one. If they wanted a fight, he figured he would give them all that he had in him and maybe then some.

The one Billy was looking at stopped, raised himself in his stirrups and waved both arms back and forth. "Yo! Vince. He's wearing a badge," he shouted. "Did you hear me? The man's wearing a badge."

"I hear," a voice came from behind. From much closer behind than Billy would have expected.

The one in front of him sat back onto his saddle and reached into his vest pocket. He produced a badge of his own and slipped it into place on the front of his vest.

"We're Texas Rangers," he announced as he kneed his horse close to Billy. "Who would you be?"

Billy introduced himself with considerable relief.

"You're one of those Mounted Agents, eh? I'd heard they were putting you boys into the field, but you're the first of them I've ever met. I'm Tom Donnelly. My partner there is Vince Weiss. Is it true that you're out looking for Chinamen?"

"It's true," Billy told them as the two Rangers dismounted and tied their horses to the whippy mesquite branches.

"There's no Chinamen around here that I know of," Weiss said.

"Not so many that want to be seen anyway," Billy said. "Fact is, I caught some of them coming across at that ford right down there. Broke up a smuggling ring that was bringing Chinese girls in for immoral purposes."

"I'll be damned. Good for you. Tell you what, though. While you're at it, I sure wish you'd do something about all the rustling been going on across both sides of the border here."

"I saw a bunch of those too," Billy told them, "but that was a couple weeks ago."

"Nothing since?"

"Nope. Just the Tibbetts bringing a bunch of stolen cows across. That first gather got away from them when they started some shooting, so they tried again a few days after. Made the mistake of coming across north of Marly where my partner was. They shot at him too, and he killed a couple of them."

"Tibbett, you said?"

"That's right."

"I know a Tibbett family from over around Beeville. You don't know if this was them, do you?"

"No. I just know the son was named Jim."

"Damn. I think that's them. Pretty good folks too."

"Jim is dead now. So is his pap, whatever his name was."

"I'm sorry to hear that. That was some weeks back, you say?"

"Yes, sir. I haven't seen hoof nor horn of any stolen stock coming across since that time. Neither has my partner, or I'm sure he would've said something to me about it."

Donnelly scratched under his chin and said, "That strikes me kinda strange because the reason we're here is all the squawking the Mexes over in Coahuila State are making. They've made formal complaints with the consul down in Mexico City, and it's got kicked up to Austin and now into our laps. They say there's a steady flow of cattle being stolen and run across the river somewhere around here."

"Not right at this ford, I can tell you," Billy said. "I've been posted right here. They aren't coming over at night when I'm in town either, for I check the crossing for tracks every morning first thing when I get here. The bank down there takes human footprints easy enough. I'd have to be blind to miss the sign of a bunch of beeves coming across."

Weiss grunted. "We didn't see any tracks neither. How about further north?"

"There's two crossings north of town. My partner watches them, just like I watch down here. Like I said, he'd've said something if there were livestock being brought over, even if it is Chinese we're supposed to be keeping out."

"All right then. I expect they could know about you Federal boys being in the area. Could be the thieves are trailing their herds further north before they bring them over. Though God knows where they've found another crossing. The next one I know about is a good forty miles north of Marly. What about you, Tom? You know of any others?"

"No. But then I don't know this country as good as you do, Vince."

"Yeah, well, we'll just have to ride on and see what we can see."

"Will you be going into Marly to spend the night?" Billy asked. He had in mind that he'd ride along with them for the company if they were headed that way. The Rangers were a likable pair, he thought. Now that they'd decided they didn't need to shoot him after all.

"No, I don't expect so. We'll move on along. Our captain is getting stung by the bigwigs in Austin, and they're getting the spurs put to them by the governor, and he's getting it from the Mexican consul. What it comes down to is that somebody better do something mighty quick." Weiss grinned. "And guess who it is that's at the bottom of the heap of all this stomping."

Billy laughed. "I think I could even tell you their names."

"You got that right, Federal man."

"I wish you luck, Vince, Tom." Billy shook hands with the two and watched them ride off to the north.

He collected his gear and started in that direction too, angling west toward Marly, though, while the Rangers went straight on to bypass the town.

FIFTY-SEVEN

"RANGERS? Where? Are they coming here?"

"No, sir," Billy told his partner. "Since we're here keeping an eye on things, they've gone upriver. I guess there's an awful lot of cow-thieving going on across the river, and the Mexican government is pushing the Texas governor to put a stop to it. That's why these two have been sent. They're looking for the crossing point now. They didn't tell me what they intend to do once they find it. Setting up an ambush maybe, like we've done to stop the Chinese traffic."

"You told them what happened here?"

"Yes, sir, I did. And of course they could see for themselves there hadn't been any cattle cross at the ford down there. None since that big rain anyhow."

Adler grunted. "All right then." After a moment he asked, "Did they say they'd be coming back?"

"No, they didn't. But I don't expect they would. There's no reason for them to now that we're watching north and south."

"You told them about that too, did you?"

"Yes, sir, of course."

"All right. That's all right." Adler pushed his plate away, leaving a good amount of his supper untouched. "I'm gonna have myself some fun tonight. D'you have enough money, boy? Want to come have some drinks with me and play a little poker?"

"No, I . . . no, thank you."

"Suit yourself." Adler stood and, as usual, headed toward the back of the place where the entertainments could be found.

Billy finished his meal and walked outside. It was dark and the air had cooled considerably after the stifling heat of the day. He liked the feel of it. He walked down by the river and stood there for a long time, peering at the stars, seeing Edith in his mind. He wished . . . it did not matter what he wished. He simply had to live with what was, not what he wanted.

Eventually, he turned away from the dark flow of the Rio Grande and headed back toward his room. As he reached the saloon, two men were coming out.

"Evenin', Agent Delisle."

"Pardon? Oh." He smiled. "I was woolgathering and didn't recognize you. Sorry. But I thought you were heading on north," he told the two Rangers.

"We decided to come back for the night," Weiss said.

"Then maybe I'll see you again in the morning." Billy started inside, but Donnelly stopped him.

"Delisle."

"Yes?"

"This partner of yours. You said he always covers the ford up north while you're always on the south side?"

"That's right. He has much more experience, so he takes the north side. There's two fords up there, you see, and he thought he ought to take responsibility for the two of them."

"Tell us about him, please."

Billy smiled. "You probably already know quite a lot about him. He's Tuck Adler, the gunfighter and lawman."

"I remember something about him being a gunfighter. Don't know about him as a lawman," Donnelly said.

"Well, he is. He knows an awful lot about outlaws and such."

"I can believe that," Weiss said. "You don't know where he is, do you?"

"He was inside here a little while ago."

"We'd like to talk to him."

"The way you say, that sounds like your talk isn't likely to be a pleasant one."

"That will depend on him," Weiss said.

"We know you're straight, Delisle," Donnelly added. "We checked the riverbank ourselves, remember? But after we left you, we went and looked at the other crossings too. There's a bunch of cattle been moved across there recently. At both places."

"The way we see it," Weiss said, "Adler is using his badge to steal cows from any rustlers that aren't in cahoots with him. His own boys he lets pass. Any others, he takes the cattle and turns them over to his crowd. We want to find out from him who he's tied in with. He'll have a choice. He can help us and get some credit with the judge when the time comes, or he can clam up and take the whole rap himself."

"But either way I'm afraid Tuck Adler is going behind bars," said Donnelly.

"Lordy," Billy blurted out. "That's why when I saw the smuggler guide he said he was on our side now. He thought I was in this deal with Mr. Adler. That means he's probably met up with the smuggler boss and struck a deal with him too. Mr. Adler could let Chinese come past him and look the other way in exchange for a payoff. Damn! No wonder I didn't see any prisoner come past me on the highway. He told me he arrested the man and turned him over to a Ranger in Tilden."

"Billy, the only Rangers assigned anywhere near Tilden in the past four months is Vince and me, and nobody turned any Federal prisoners over to us."

"Damn it anyway," Billy moaned.

"We're going to check the other saloons on the street here, then go across to the Mex side if we can't find him here. If you see him, Billy, come get us. We can handle him."

The implication, Billy realized, was that the Rangers did not believe Billy Delisle could handle Tuck Adler.

And of course they were right.

"I . . . I'm sorry, fellas. I am truly sorry."

"You didn't do it, Delisle. We know that."

"But I sure feel stupid. And responsible. After all, I'm wearing this badge too. Now Mr. Adler has gone and tarnished it."

"Remember what we said. If you see him, come tell us. We'll take him in."

"Right. I remember what you said."

"Good." The two Texas Rangers touched the brims of their hats and walked off into the night.

Billy shivered even though the air was far from being cold.

The thing was . . . he knew perfectly good and well where Mr. Adler would be right now if he wasn't still in the saloon.

Billy had no intention of telling the Rangers that, though.

He shivered again. Then went inside.

FIFTY-EIGHT

"COME in."

Billy took a deep breath, then lifted the latch and entered Tuck Adler's room behind the saloon. Adler was there, where he pretty much always was once he left the gaming tables, with one of the plump whores who shared their earnings with the saloon.

This one was wearing only black silk stockings and her high-lace shoes. She looked like she belonged on one of those back-bar paintings. Billy saw she was there, but kept his attention on Mr. Adler. He'd had more than enough to do with whores already.

Adler was standing beside the bed with his coat off and shirt unbuttoned. He had removed his underarm holsters. They, with his guns still in them, were hung on the back of a small chair an arm's length away from where he stood.

"Change your mind about partying tonight, boy? No? You look mighty serious. What is it?"

"Those Rangers came back."

"Oh?"

"They went by the fords up north."

"Is that a fact now."

"Yes, sir, it is. They've figured out what you've been doing. About the cattle, I mean. I'm the one who knew about the smuggling ring. You threw in with them too, didn't you?"

"Did I? You seem to know every damn thing. You tell me."

"Yes, sir. I expect that you did at that."

Adler was carefully buttoning his shirt back to the top. He reached for the guns, but only took them by the straps and shrugged into the harness, tying them down with purpose-made cords that went to buttons sewn onto the waistbands of his britches for just that reason. "Remember what I told you, boy. Life is short. Enjoy it while you can. That's my philosophy. That's what I do."

"You're a thief, Mr. Adler. I looked up to you, but you're only a thief."

"Sure I am. But at least I'm a man. You, you aren't nothing but a queer."

"Pardon me?"

"You don't know what to call it? Queer. Bugger boy. Brown-poler. Is that clearer to you?"

"What the hell are you talking about?"

"You hide it pretty good, boy, but Carmen told me what you did that night you were with her. Said you wouldn't touch her. Just sat there mumbling about somebody called Eddie. Shit. Left your lover boy back in El Paso, did you?

You're damned lucky you didn't make the mistake of reaching for me. I'd've shot you right in the crotch." Adler checked to see that his Colts were free in the leather, then pulled his coat on so that he was fully dressed.

"Thinking of shooting you, boy. I expect you'd best step outa that doorway because I think it's time I take a little sashay out of here and across the border."

Billy scarcely heard. "Carmen. That was the whore you sent to the room with me a while back?"

"Yes of course. Were you too drunk to remember her name?"

Billy grinned. He felt like the weight of the world had just been lifted off his shoulders. "As a matter of fact, I guess I was that drunk. All I did was talk about Eddie, huh?"

"That's right, and I've not had any respect for you since. I got no use for queers."

"Thank you for telling me that. It makes me feel a lot better."

"Now ain't that just sweet. Now step aside, boy. I want to get across that bridge before the Rangers come back here."

"No, sir, I can't do that."

"What? Billy boy, don't you remember who I am? Do you know how many men I've killed? Grown men. Good men with a gun. Well, bad men mostly. But good with their guns. There's nobody can stand up to me in a face-to-face fight, and I don't figure to show you my back when I walk outa here. Now move aside. I got to go."

Billy stood with his back to the door. He shifted his feet a little apart so as to brace himself.

"I've got proud of this badge we both wear, Tuck. I won't let you sully it."

"You'd die for that, boy?"

"I'm no boy, Tuck. And I'm not gonna move."

"You called me by my first name. You've never done that before, boy."

"I guess there comes a first time for most everything."

"Including dying if you don't stand aside and let me walk out of this room. Now move. I have to go."

Billy took a deep breath.

He stood where he was, unmoving.

FIFTY-NINE

MR. Adler would shoot him. Billy had no doubt about that. The man would shoot him down and step over his body and saunter easy as you please across to Mexico and freedom. And the only person who could stop him was one William Anders Delisle.

Billy's heart was racing, but his determination was steady. He was *not* going to move. Not if he died for it, he wouldn't.

He knew what to expect. Mr. Adler's Colts would flash into his hands quick as a wink and . . .

Maybe. Maybe there was a way.

Billy tried to slow his breathing. He swallowed. Hard.

"Tuck, I am placing you under arrest."

Adler laughed. Tossed his head back and brayed. "Did you hear that?" he asked the doxy, who was cowering on the bed behind him. "The pup is barking like a full-grown dog." Adler's expression turned hard. "That don't make you anything other than a pup," he said. "Now I'm giving you one last chance. Step out of my way or I'll shoot you down and walk right over you."

Billy had heard all about old-time chivalry and about the gunfighter's code that the dime novels talked about, how the bad man was supposed to go for his gun first and the hero be the quicker.

Well, bullshit with that notion. There wasn't anybody anywhere who didn't know that Tuck Adler was faster than most anybody. For damn certain faster than some boy off a hardscrabble ranch in New Mexico who'd never in his life fired a shot at anything other than a paper target or a clod of dirt.

Waiting was just going to get him dead, and that did not strike him as a very good idea.

Adler took a step forward and while he was on one foot and moving, Billy grabbed for the butt of his .44 Smith and Wesson.

His fingers barely had time to touch the wood of the grips before Adler had one of his Colts out.

Billy stood and concentrated on what he had to do.

Never mind what the gunfighter was doing. That was the only edge Billy had. Steadiness would have to substitute for speed. And if he calculated this wrong, well, he wouldn't live long enough to worry about regrets afterward.

His hand closed on the Smith and he yanked it out of the leather.

Adler's .45 roared. The sound inside the small rented room was louder than a Fourth of July cannon shot. There was smoke and flame, and Adler's bullet came close enough that Billy could feel the breath of its passage.

Probably he would have heard the zing of it going past if he hadn't already been deafened.

He tried his best to ignore all that, swinging his Smith into line, his concentration on the row of Adler's shirt buttons. That was where he would have to aim.

Adler's second shot crashed out inside the close confinement, and Billy's nostrils were filled with the stink of the burnt powder. His ears rang from the concussion, and his eyes stung from the acrid smoke of the first shot.

Two shots. That was what Adler had told him. Two shots to unnerve his opponent, then try to hit with the third.

Billy started to squeeze the trigger of the Smith.

He dropped to one knee as he did so, and Adler's third shot zipped inches over Billy's head.

The .44-40 Smith bucked in his hand, its sound lost amid the ear-ringing from Adler's firing.

Billy knew he wasn't fast, but then a fast noise couldn't hurt you. And he'd learned to be accurate even if he couldn't be fast.

A dark spot appeared on the front of Adler's shirt just to the left of his third button.

Adler fired again, but toward the floor.

The gunfighter looked puzzled about something. As if he couldn't figure out what was going wrong here.

Billy aimed. Once again squeezed the double-action trigger. The Smith roared.

Tuck Adler gave Billy a disbelieving look and shook his head minutely, the movement barely discernible.

Then Mounted Agent—and thief—Tucker Adler dropped to his knees.

He stayed there, swaying from side to side, for only a moment.

Then he toppled forward facedown on the hard-packed earthen floor.

Behind him, the Mexican whore was screaming. Billy could tell that she was because he could see her mouth open and the quivering of her throat, but he was so deafened by the resounding gunfire that he could not hear her screams.

He looked at Tuck Adler, whose blood was beginning to flow onto the floor beneath his body. Billy opened the cylinder of the Smith and—just as his mentor Tuck Adler had taught him—immediately reloaded the gun before returning it to its holster.

Then he turned and went to look for the Texas Rangers.

SIXTY

My dearest darling Edith:
 Please forgive me. I love you. I have always loved
you and I always shall. It will be difficult to explain
to you the reasons for my recent foolishness, but
before I even attempt to do that I must beg for your
forgiveness. I have caused you distress, you who are
the most beloved of women.
 I mu

He placed his pen aside and thought for a moment.
Then he pushed himself away from the table and strode
rapidly across the room to the bar.

"Nelson."

"Yes, Mr. Delisle?"

"I have work to do here yet, but first I have to go away
for a few weeks. I want you to hold my room for me. And

look after my gear. I'll be leaving it there. See that nothing is disturbed while I'm gone." He smiled, probably for the first time since he spoke to Donnelly and Weiss. "I have to go see a young lady about an engagement ring, you see."

The bartender grinned. "In that case, sir, let me be the first to offer congratulations."

Sir. It wasn't until Billy was halfway out to his room that he realized Nelson called him "sir."

Billy didn't think anyone had ever said that to him before.

It felt odd.

But kind of nice actually.

His heart began racing now even faster than when he'd taken a gun and faced Tuck Adler.

Edith. He was going home to see Edith.

Going so he could explain.

Going so he could hold her in his arms. Bury his face in her hair. Kiss her sweet lips and hear her dear voice.

Then, dammit, he would come back to Marly and find John Smith so he could finish up the job Adler had failed to do and break up this ring that smuggled Chinese.

But first . . .

Edie was waiting.

LINGO BARNES IS ON HIS WAY TO DURANGO,
COLORADO, WHEN HE STUMBLES UPON THE KIDNAPPING
OF EMILY LOU COLTER. NOW HE MUST SAVE THE GIRL
AND KEEP HIMSELF OUT OF THE LINE OF FIRE.

JUSTICE HAS A NEW HOME.

HANGING VALLEY

No one knows the American West better than

JACK BALLAS

Author of *West of the River*

0-425-18410-2

BERKLEY